THE NORDLINGS

THE
NORDLINGS

by

Kathleen McDonnell

SECOND
STORY
Press

CANADIAN CATALOGUING IN PUBLICATION DATA

McDonnell, Kathleen, 1947–
The nordlings

ISBN 1-896764-23-1

I. Title

PS8575.D669N67 1999   jC813'.54   C99-931764-4
PZ7.M32No 1999

Edited by Catherine Marjoribanks
Cover illustration by Kasia Charko

*Second Story Press gratefully acknowledges the assistance of the
Ontario Arts Council and the Canada Council for the Arts
for our publishing program. We acknowledge the financial
support of the Government of Canada through the
Book Publishing Industry Development Program
for our publishing activities.*

Canadä

Printed and bound in Canada

Published by
SECOND STORY PRESS
*720 Bathurst Street, Suite 301
Toronto Canada M5S 2R4*

Contents

I travel'd thro' a Land of Men
A Land of Men and Women too,
And heard and saw such dreadful things
As cold Earth wanderers never knew.

— from "The Mental Traveller"
by William Blake

Prologue

"ANOTHER ONE GONE!" he said, after they had searched everywhere for the tiny creature. "Are you satisfied now?"

Mi* had never seen the two of them fight. Bicker, yes. All the time. But not this kind of cold fury, with Gavi's black-and-white feathers bristling and the hard glint in Molly's good eye. The creeping, day-to-day terror of life in Notherland was bad enough. But now the sight of the two most important people in her world so angry at one another frightened Mi.

"It was you who kept me from going after the Nobodaddy right at the start!"

"Shhh! Not in front of her!" the loon said harshly, gesturing towards Mi.

But it was too late. The long, strange name was out, a name with more sounds than Mi had ever heard.

"Stop being foolish!" Gavi commanded. "We cannot do it alone. We have to try to bring her back. There is no other way."

"Just what makes you think she'd even care?" Molly shot back. "The great Pay-gee acts like she doesn't even know we exist anymore!"

Mi was shocked. How dare Molly say the name of the great

---

* The name Mi is taken from the third note of the musical scale and is pronounced Me.

Creator of Notherland in such a disdainful tone of voice!

But Gavi's reply was even more startling.

"If we do nothing, we will cease to exist. Our whole world will be wiped out in the blink of an eye. Is that what you want?"

Gavi's words rang in her head, and Mi felt a shudder course through her tiny body.

CHAPTER 1

Around Again

"You're doing what?"

Peggy had stuffed the flute case way down in her knapsack, hoping her mom wouldn't notice, so she could get out of the house without a big scene. But no such luck.

"Have you completely lost your mind?"

How does she always know? Peggy wondered. *It's like she can smell when something's up.*

"Oh please, don't freak out ..."

"Why would you want to do that?"

"For money, why else? I'm tired of being broke all the time!"

"But you can't go selling a thing like that!"

"Why not? It's mine. I can do what I want with it."

"Oh, really? And what would your father say about that?"

Now Peggy exploded. "What should I care what he thinks? He doesn't have anything to do with my life anymore!"

She stormed out of the apartment.

"Fine, go ahead, sell it!" her mother yelled down the hall after her. "I'm tired of arguing with you. Sell your soul for all I care!"

'Sell your soul'? Peggy thought. *Give me a break.*

She couldn't wait to finally turn sixteen. Then that witch wouldn't be able to tell her what to do!

❖

Peggy was amazed that the idea hadn't occurred to her before. She'd walked by that pawnshop a couple of weeks ago. In the window, wedged in between a full-length mirror and an old upright vacuum cleaner, she'd seen a flute sitting in a velvet-lined case, the same make as hers. She'd glanced at the price tag: $800.

Then, a few days later, she was watching a commercial on TV and it all came together in her head.

"Bring your used goods to Around Again — and walk out with cold, hard cash!"

The ad showed a steady stream of people walking through a revolving door, carrying cameras and other things, and then coming out clutching handfuls of money. It was an ad she'd seen dozens of times, but this time she noticed something: one of the men went in carrying a saxophone. A musical instrument ...

Her mind flashed back instantly to the flute in the window.

Eight hundred dollars ...

She was flabbergasted to think she actually owned something that was worth that kind of money. Okay, maybe she couldn't expect to get that much, but the flute in the pawnshop was the exact same make as hers. If she took hers in, they'd have to offer her at least something close ...

Eight hundred bucks!

Why not? She hardly ever played it anymore. She'd skipped almost every orchestra rehearsal since the beginning of school. What was she holding on to it for?

What would your father say?

So what? He was gone, he was out of her life. Sure, she'd spent all those years playing, practising, and she'd even kept it up for a long time after he left. But now the thought took a clear and simple shape in her mind: *I don't have to play anymore. I can do what I want!*

She could go places, get stuff, buy clothes. With that kind of money, she could even start saving up to move out on her own. By this time next year, she'd be sixteen. She'd have her own life. And finally get out from under her mom's thumb!

Eight hundred bucks!

The flute was her ticket to freedom!

✧

The store was ringed by a long counter divided into sections, with the items for sale grouped on shelves behind it. Peggy looked around until she saw some instruments — several guitars, a couple of accordions, some brass horns.

No flutes?

Was that a bad sign? Maybe flutes didn't sell. Then again, maybe they sold quickly ...

She placed her black flute case on the counter. The salesman looked expectantly in her direction.

"I was wondering how much I could get for this ..." she said hesitantly. She snapped up the clasps, opened the case and turned it towards him.

"Depends on the make," he said, walking over to look at it, "the condition it's in."

"Oh, it's in great condition ..." Peggy began.

The salesman picked up two sections of the flute and now looked quizzically inside the case.

"Where's the rest of it?"

"What do you mean?"

"The mouthpiece," he said. "It's not here."

"What?"

He whirled the case around towards her. It was empty! Where was the mouthpiece?

"It was in there!"

The salesman just looked at her and shrugged.

Could she have left it behind, in the rush to pack up and get past her mom?

"I must've left it at home. Look, I can go right back and get it. Could you just tell me how much you'll give me for it?"

"Not until I see the whole thing."

"Please, just give me some idea?"

The man shook his head. "Look, honey, how do you expect me to do a proper appraisal without the mouthpiece?"

Peggy sighed. "All right, fine. I'll be back in half an hour." She turned to go.

"Wait," the man called after her. "You're not going to just leave this here, are you?" He held up the flute case. "That wouldn't be very smart, now would it? I might just decide to hold on to it. Then you wouldn't get a penny."

He chuckled as she walked back towards the revolving door, the flute case under her arm.

I am such an idiot!

She couldn't believe it. She'd carried the case all the way back to the subway, boarded a train, flopped down onto a seat and gone half a dozen stops before she'd opened her knapsack to put the case back in. And there was the mouthpiece, sitting smack at the bottom of the knapsack, almost as though it was mocking her.

Why didn't I look in here before I left the store?

Okay, fine. All she had to do was get off the train, change platforms and head back in the other direction to Around Again.

The train was just pulling into a station. She bounded off the car and headed towards the escalator. Then she saw the large block letters on the concrete wall in front of her: GREEN ECHO PARK. Her mouth dropped open.

Huh?

Green Echo Park was way out in the west end. She'd taken the wrong train!

What is with me today? I can't do anything right!

Of all the stations, it would have to be this one, she thought. *It's just too funny.*

She went up the escalator and paused at the top. A sign on the wall ahead said EXIT TO PARK ROAD, with an arrow pointing to the left.

It had been more than four years since she'd set foot on that street.

✧

Peggy shivered in her blue fleece jacket as she emerged from the subway. It had been fairly mild through the first couple of weeks of December, but in the past few days the temperature had dropped. She started walking up Park Road, and gratefully enjoyed the warmth of the sunlight. On one side of the street was Green Echo Park, with a line of benches bordering the sidewalk. On the other side, front doors facing the park, was a row of houses.

As soon as she spied the familiar red brick, she felt a ripple of surprise. Of course it was still there. What had she expected? She'd managed to push that whole time right out of her mind, but that didn't mean the house had stopped existing. Someone else was living there now. Some other family.

She looked at the window into the music room, where, from the time she was seven, she had practised every day, without exception. At first just piano, but when she'd turned ten, and her father decided that her fingers were long enough, he'd started her on the flute.

From the beginning she had to practise piano for an hour at a time. When she took up the flute, he added another hour. Her mother tried to object that Peggy was too young, but he insisted — that was the minimum she needed to make progress. And her mom caved in to him, as usual.

"Peggy doesn't mind, do you sweetheart?" he said. "What's the point of learning an instrument if you're not going to be any good? Right?"

Peggy would nod her head eagerly.

Often he'd come into the music room while she was practising, close the door and just sit listening, a smile on his face.

"The boys and your mother, they're not like you and me," he'd tell her confidentially. "They have no ear for music."

She loved it when he said things like that. It made her light up inside.

But there were the other times, too. Like when he'd overhear a mistake and come tearing into the room, yelling, "What's the matter with you? You've played that piece a hundred times. Can't you do anything right?"

What would your father say?

Her mom was right about one thing, at least: he would never have let her out of the house with the flute. He would've ripped into her but good. He would've gone totally berserk. He would've physically stopped her from leaving.

But why should she worry now? He lived five hundred miles away. She hadn't even talked to him in more than two years. Why was her stomach getting all tied up in a knot?

What are you hanging around here for? Get your butt back to Around Again!

As Peggy turned to head back to the subway, her eye was drawn to the park entrance, just across the street. An old-fashioned wrought-iron gate, always open, was set back a bit from the street, and just inside it a pathway wound around the base of a large stone statue.

That angel ...

She went over to take a closer look.

The statue had a pair of enormous stone wings folded in front of it in a near-semicircle. Enfolded in its wings, so that from certain angles they were almost completely hidden from view, were the likenesses of two tiny children, a boy and a girl, their faces turned upward towards the angel's. The statue was a memorial to a woman by the name of Wilma Blake, who had once operated an orphanage on the same site, over a century ago. At the base of the statue was a plaque, with the inscription: "As befits the noble name of Wilma, she was for the children of this city a Resolute Protector." Peggy recalled how, when she was in third or fourth grade, she had looked up the word "resolute" in her Junior Dictionary. It meant "determined, bold, firm of purpose."

As she stood gazing up at the statue she heard a sharp swoosh! Inside the park, she could just make out the upper bodies of several figures gliding in smooth, circular motions.

Skaters!

Peggy was amazed that it was cold enough for ice. But she remembered that the pond in Green Echo Park was shallow and used to freeze over early in the season. She hadn't put on her skates once since they'd moved away from here, but now the sensation came back to her in a sudden rush — the glorious sense of gliding effortlessly along on that perfectly smooth ice. She remembered hearing someone say that skating was the closest thing to flying without leaving the earth, and thinking, *Yes! That's exactly what it feels like! Flying!*

❖

"There she is ..."

"So close ..."

"She's not moving! She's just standing there, looking! If she doesn't make a move soon I swear I'll reach out and pull her through that gate!"

Gavi drew one of his wings over Molly's head, causing her rigid body to tumble over backwards.

"What'd'ya do that for?"

"To keep you from doing something stupid." Gavi pulled his wing back, allowing the indignant doll to jump back to her feet. "Do you want to ruin everything?"

The two of them were standing at the edge of Painted Rock, a smooth rock face that stretched along the shore of Lake Notherland. From a distance, it looked like ordinary stone with a few reddish-brown figures etched into it. But up close, its surface looked almost transparent, and shadowy objects could be seen moving on the other side.

Gavi and Molly had always taken great pains to keep the Nordlings away from Painted Rock. It was the place where the boundary between Notherland and the other realm — the world of the Creator — was nearly paper-thin. Chaos might result if someone accidentally tumbled through. Just on the other side of Painted Rock was a small hill ringed by trees. This was where Notherland had first come into being, the passageway to the world of the Creator.

"What if she just stands there?" Molly demanded. "What if she turns around and never even sets foot on that mound? Then we've gone through all this for nothing!"

"You have no idea what might happen if you go barrelling through that rock," Gavi replied sternly. "You cannot take the chance. We must be patient."

"I hate being patient!" Molly exploded. "I want to do something!"

◆

Peggy's thoughts were interrupted by nearby voices. A couple of boys were approaching the park gate, each with a pair of skates dangling from his shoulders. They seemed to be calling over to a third person Peggy couldn't see.

"Well, if it isn't Scary Gary!"

"Hey, Gary! How ya doin' today?"

They both laughed, and a low grunt came from behind the statue.

Curious, Peggy walked past the wrought-iron gate to see who it was they were talking to.

Someone was sitting at the base of the statue. His back was to Peggy and he was slumped over so she couldn't see his face. Despite the weather, he wasn't wearing a jacket, just some worn jeans, a sweatshirt and badly scuffed boots with the soles coming away. The only thing that didn't look like it had come from the dollar-a-pound bin at the Salvation Army was a mustard-coloured leather vest. The leather was dirty and scuffed, but on the back of the vest was a beautiful, intricately designed tree done in beadwork.

Now he lifted his head a bit, and she could see that he was fairly young, close to her own age. He looked like one of those kids from the Native reserves up north. She sometimes saw them panhandling downtown, but she was surprised to find one of them here, in this part of town, in Green Echo Park.

In one hand he was clutching a brown paper bag. Peggy watched as he lowered his head and pressed his face into it. The sides of the bag flapped in and out with each breath, like a stiff balloon.

One of the boys laughed again.

"Hey, Gary. Can we have a sniff?"

He just grunted again, more irascibly this time.

"Aw, c'mon, Gary. Just a little one ..."

Peggy was a bit startled to hear her own voice, in a snappish tone.

"Why don't you leave him alone?" she said to the boys. "He's not bothering you."

They looked at her in surprise.

"We're just kidding around," one of them said.

"Yeah," the other added, with a slight smirk on his face. "He doesn't mind. Do you, Gary?"

This time Gary made no response, and the two boys laughed as they brushed past Peggy on their way out the park gate.

Peggy looked into the young man's face, but though he stared right at her, his eyes had an utterly empty expression, as though he had no awareness of her or anything else around him.

Nobody home in there, Peggy thought uneasily. She felt a wave of pity for him as he again slumped over, leaning against the statue. She remembered how, when she was little, she used to stand there at the base of the statue and feel such a longing to be enfolded in the angel's wings, to hear the angel say in a gentle whisper, "Don't be afraid. You are safe here."

I'd better get out of here, she thought, with a shiver. *This place is starting to get to me.*

❖

"Oh, no!" Gavi cried.

"What is it?"

"It looks like she is heading the other way again. I thought we were in like Flynn!"

"Huh? Who's Flynn?" Molly asked.

"It is a human expression," Gavi said impatiently. "It means — oh, never mind!"

"What do we do now?"

"I do not know," Gavi said, with desperation in his voice. "I must think!"

"Well, you think all you want. I'm not going to sit here and watch all our effort go to waste!"

Molly hadn't told Gavi of her plan. She knew how nervous he got at the very idea of breaching the boundary between the two universes. But now she decided the time had come to play her trump card.

The loon watched in stupefaction as, clutching an object in her fist, she raised her arm.

"What are you doing? No, Molly! No!"

Before he could do a thing to stop her, she'd lobbed the object right in the direction of Painted Rock, into which it appeared to be swallowed up completely.

❖

It was the oddest thing.

As she was turning back towards the park entrance, Peggy caught sight of a ring of poplar trees farther inside the park, out of which an object appeared to flip right up into the air and fall back down again.

Did someone throw something? She looked around. Other than Gary, still slumped down on the other side of the statue, there was no one around. Even the pond was empty of skaters.

She walked towards the ring of trees, which surrounded a small mound of earth. She scrambled up onto it and looked around. At first she saw nothing, but then, at the base of one of the trees, she spied a silvery object. It was a small silver spoon — very old, quite tarnished, decorated with intricate metalwork tendrils. She picked it up.

Where have I seen this spoon before?

Suddenly an image of startling clarity popped into her head: a full-colour portrait of Sir John Franklin, the great Arctic explorer. She could even read the caption underneath: "Franklin went missing in 1847 and was never heard from again." Then another illustration: "Franklin's devoted wife, Lady Jane Franklin, who commissioned many rescue missions in an ultimately fruitless search for her husband." Beneath that caption was a grainy reproduction of an old photograph of an antique silver spoon and chipped tea cup: "Objects found on the arctic tundra, believed to be relics of the long-lost Franklin expedition."

That book! She used to spend hours paging through it, looking at the pictures, reading parts of it over and over again.

What was it called? Something about the North ...

❖

"Are you ready?"

"Ready!"

"One ... Two ... Three ..."
Their voices joined in unison.
"PULL NOW!"

✦

Suddenly Peggy felt disoriented. The earth underneath her started to feel soft, spongy, as if it were about to give way. She struggled to regain her footing, but the ground shifted violently, and then caved in completely.

She had a strong sensation of being pulled down, and of a hand gripping her arm. For a moment she even thought she saw a face pressing up against hers, a smooth face with a black patch over one eye. She wanted to scream in terror, but when she opened her mouth no sound came out, like in a dream.

Then everything went dark ...

CHAPTER 2

The Creator

"IN THE SUMMER MONTHS, the sun never sets in the far North. And throughout the year the sky is lit up by a steady glow from luminous bands of light that seem to shoot up towards the heavens. These are the famous Northern Lights, a phenomenon also known by its Greek name Aurora Borealis. In the folklore of Northern peoples, the lights of the 'RoryBory' are sometimes regarded as the souls of departed loved ones, or as fairies or sprites. Some Arctic dwellers even say they can hear the Northern Lights 'singing.'"

Seven-year-old Peggy spent hours poring over Our Wondrous North. It had quite a few big words, but she was a good reader and could sound them out, or figure out the meaning from the pictures. And it was the pictures she loved most — of tall pine forests, of loons swimming on sparkling, clear lakes, of the blazing RoryBory itself.

Imagine, she thought to herself: a land where there is no darkness. Bad feelings come with the night, but if the night never comes ... It was comforting to think there might be such a place. Lying in bed hugging her doll Molly, Peggy tried to picture it in her mind: the land of the RoryBory, where darkness never came. But it was difficult. She needed more than pictures to go on.

She sat up in bed, leaned over and pressed her face — and Molly's — to the window looking out over the park. Suppose the pond was stretched out so it was the size of a big Northern lake. Suppose instead of ducks there were loons swimming around on the lake. Suppose the stumpy trees that ringed the little hill were tall pine trees. And suppose near the edge of that pond that was really a lake, by that ring of trees that was really a pine forest, there was a big, smooth rock ...

✧

Peggy landed with a thud, almost as if she'd jerked awake after nodding off to sleep. She sat upright and blinked. The blackness lifted like a veil. She could see again.

What happened? Did I pass out?

She gently shook her head to clear it. As she struggled to her feet, she noticed that her knapsack felt much lighter than before. She swung the pack off her back and saw that the top flap had somehow come open. She reached inside and rifled around.

Empty. Her flute case was gone! Frantic, she looked around to see where it might have fallen out and saw ...

What the ...?

She was no longer surrounded by the same ring of trees. They seemed to have straightened out into a row of tall pines, stretching far into the distance. The pond seemed to have grown much larger, too — so large she couldn't see across to the far shore. She was startled to see ripples on the water.

Water? There was ice there a minute ago!

She heard a fluttering noise and turned in the direction it came from. A black-and-white bird was flapping its wings along the surface of the water. It wasn't one of the Green Echo Park ducks, though. It was larger, more the size of a goose.

Am I dreaming?

It looked to Peggy as though the bird was trying to get airborne, but instead of taking off, it scurried towards the shore. Then, to Peggy's utter astonishment, the bird walked right out of the water.

"It worked! I knew you would come."

Peggy looked all around, but she could see no one. She'd heard the voice as plain as day. Where had it come from?

"Welcome back, Peggy. We missed you."

At the sound of her name Peggy whirled around again, but this time there was no mistaking where the voice was coming from.

"A talking bird," she said out loud. "Oh, I'm in dreamland, all right."

"You never used to think there was anything unusual about my talking," the bird replied in a slightly wounded tone of voice. "And I must say, I am a bit insulted. How could you confuse our beautiful Notherland, the most superior of all universes, with a mundane place like 'dreamland'?"

Peggy looked at the bird in stupefaction, as if it were babbling gibberish instead of speaking perfectly comprehensible English.

He shook his head. "You really do not remember, do you?"

Peggy was startled by the sound of another voice coming from behind her.

"See? What'd I tell you?"

She turned to see a smallish creature with the size and appearance of a seven- or eight-year-old child, but with arms and legs that were strangely rigid and a black patch covering one eye.

"We might as well never have existed, as far as she's concerned!" the odd-looking child continued. "To think how she used to go on and on about how much she loved me —"

"You!" Peggy interrupted her. "That ..." she sputtered, pointing to the patch. But she couldn't put two words together.

"Do you remember now?" the strange child asked sternly, walking over to Peggy and looking her square in the face. "Do you remember *me*?"

Peggy stared hard into the face of the child — and realized with a start that this was, in fact, a doll she was speaking to. Her doll. Molly.

"This," she said slowly, "cannot be happening ..."

Gavi came over and touched her hand with a gentle flutter of one wing.

"Oh," he said softly, "but it is."

✧

"On smooth rock faces on many Northern lakes are found pictographs, paintings of animals such as deer, bear, caribou and other creatures. These drawings were made long ago by Native people, who believed that the spirits of these creatures lived within the rocks.

Like the raths or fairy mounds in European folk tales, pictograph rocks could serve as passageways into other, unseen worlds."

Little Peggy closed Our Wondrous North *and lay back in her bed. Daydreaming about the Other Land where darkness never came, telling Molly about it — it just didn't seem like enough anymore. She wanted to go there, to see it for herself. She sat up and looked out her window. Suppose the little hill in the park across the street was really one of those fairy mounds. Suppose that smooth rock in the Other Land was one of those Painted Rocks, like the ones in* Our Wondrous North. *And suppose you could use it to go back and forth between this world and the Other Land ...*

❖

"She does look a bit different now, but still like herself."

"Of course she looks different. She is older now, more grown-up."

They were talking about her.

"You two are *exactly* as I remember you!" Peggy blurted out.

It was true: Gavi had the same sleekly feathered body and lumbering movements. She'd found his name when she looked up "loon" in a field guide in the school library: *"Gavia Immer"* it said underneath the picture.

Peggy had decided it wouldn't be practical for Gavi not to be able to walk on land, like real loons. But she did make him clumsy and slow-moving, as well as a bit larger than a normal-sized loon, so he'd be more like a friend than a pet. As for his stiff, formal way of speaking, she couldn't remember how it came to be that way. He'd just spoken that way the first time he opened his mouth, and that was that.

Molly, too, was exactly the same. The lifelike plastic doll with movable arms and legs and a head that turned side to side, had been transformed, once in Notherland, into a play-mate for seven-year-old Peggy — though still with some of the same doll-like stiffness in her movements. And, of course, the patch over her missing left eye.

❖

Where had it gone?

She had looked everywhere for Molly's missing eye. After she'd got that crack in her head, her eye kept coming loose, and Peggy had to keep putting it back in place. Now it had disappeared completely. Peggy had looked everywhere she could think of. What a bad doll-mother she was. How could she have let this happen to Molly? She tried to make a kind of patch out of some torn doll clothes, to cover up the cavity and the crack beside it.

Her brothers snickered.

"Why don't you get rid of that old doll? It's a hunk of junk."

Peggy clutched Molly tightly to her chest.

"She's not junk! She's a pirate!"

The boys laughed even harder.

"Yeah! Right! Who ever heard of a doll being a pirate!"

She'd show them. She'd take Molly with her to the place she'd named Notherland. Here she was just a doll, but there she could be a walking, talking pirate doll. No one would laugh at her. No one would make fun of her missing eye. Anything was possible in the Notherland.

❖

"Then how come we aren't any different?" Molly was asking.

"Because, unlike Peggy, we do not grow older," the loon replied. "Nothing does, here in Notherland. Everything is always the same — "

"Hold on just a second," Peggy interrupted the loon. "You mean to tell me that ... we're in Notherland? Right now?"

They both nodded.

"But that's not possible."

"Oh?"

"Of course not! Notherland's just a place I made up when I was a little kid! How can it still be here? How can you still be here?"

Gavi began to clear his throat.

"He's been waiting for you to ask that question," Molly said, rolling her eyes.

"Yes, there is no doubt that you are the Creator. That is the First Great Truth of Notherland. But —"

Molly couldn't help interrupting. "Here we go —"

"Just because some of us have no interest in matters of philosophy doesn't mean —"

"Did you say 'natters'?" Molly broke in again. She turned to Peggy. "Because when he gets going, that's all he does: natter, natter, natter —"

"Excuse me!" Gavi said, with considerably more sharpness than Peggy could recall him showing in the old days. "I was speaking! Peggy here has asked a question of great import, and I am attempting to answer it."

"Oh, fine!" Molly went off in a huff. She picked up some

tiny stones and flung them, one by one, into the lake.

"As I was saying," Gavi resumed, "you are the one who created Notherland, who called it into existence, so to speak. But since then Notherland has changed."

"Changed?" asked Peggy, trying her best to take in what the loon was saying.

"In the early days of its existence, when it was what I like to call a 'baby universe,' Notherland was totally dependent on you and your imagination. But just as a baby, having been given life and sustenance by its mother, gradually moves out on its own, so does a baby universe grow to eventually take on a life that is independent of its Creator's. So Notherland has outgrown its old boundaries. It is no longer exclusively yours. It has a life of its own."

"You're running on too long, as usual!" Molly broke in. "It'll be dark soon."

"Dark?" Peggy was finally able to get a word in edgewise. "It doesn't get dark in Notherland!"

"Shows how much you know!" the doll said indignantly. She turned back to Gavi. "We have to go get her."

"Get who?" Peggy asked irritably. "Who else is there?"

Gavi and Molly looked at one another.

"Wait a minute — I know. I had a feeling something was missing. The Nordlings! Where are they?"

"I'm afraid ... you cannot see them right now," said Gavi carefully.

"Why not?"

"Because they are not here."

❖

"It's no fun anymore!"

Peggy sighed. Molly was getting in one of her moods again. The doll was certainly harder to deal with in Notherland than she was back in the other world. In Peggy's room she just sat quietly on the bed. But here, Molly was more like another kid — fun, but sometimes annoying, too.

"What's no fun?" Peggy asked her.

"We can only play games for three. It's no fun anymore."

Peggy was all set to try and explain to Molly, in her calmest, most adult voice, why they would have to make do with games for three when Gavi suddenly piped up.

"I have an idea."

Uh-oh. Another one of Gavi's ideas. He was having them more and more lately. Always thinking of ways to make Notherland better. Some of them didn't work out — like making up a whole flock of loons for the lake. They were just too noisy, wailing and flapping around on the water all the time. She made them disappear, once Gavi had decided that, since loons were territorial birds, he should be the only loon in Notherland.

But Gavi had also come up with the idea for the Great Skyway up to the RoryBory, and that had turned out to be a lot of fun.

"What's your idea?" Peggy asked.

"Playmates," Gavi said with a twinkle in his red eye. "Remember what your book said about fairies and sprites?"

Peggy saw immediately what Gavi was after. Yes, of course. It was perfect.

"What a great idea!"

Even Molly got caught up in the excitement.

Peggy closed her eyes. The others could think up the ideas, but *they couldn't make them happen. That was Peggy's job.*

"I can sort of see them," she told the two of them after a few moments. "They're like rays of light but shaped like children, and smaller than we are."

"What else?" Gavi asked.

"I think I hear something ... Yeah! They're singing!"

"What?" Molly asked excitedly.

"It's not exactly a song ..." Peggy struggled to explain. "It's more like each one has a note to sing, and they put them together in different ways. It's beautiful! But it's not like any music I've heard before."

Musical notes began to swirl around in her head, up and down the scales, just as they did when she'd practised the piano: Do-Re-Mi-Fa-Sol-La-Ti-Do-Ti-La-Sol-Fa-Mi-Re Do ...

❖

"What do you mean, 'they're not here'?"

The loon lowered his head.

"They are ... gone."

"Gone? Where?"

"So many have gone missing we have lost count ..."

"What are you talking about?" Peggy said impatiently. "There are only eight of them."

Molly threw up her hands in exasperation. "See? She knows nothing about us anymore!"

Gavi turned to Peggy, "There are many, many more Nordlings than when you were here. At least, there *were*, until the disappearances. You see, Molly wanted more company, and I began to feel that a proper universe should have more than eight notes in its musical scale— high and low notes, sharps, flats, blue notes —"

"Hold on. Are you trying to tell me ..." Peggy did her best to speak calmly, "that you created more Nordlings?"

Gavi nodded.

"How? I thought I was the only one who could do that."

"You weren't here!" Molly said scornfully. "We didn't know if you were ever coming back! What were we supposed to do?"

"Okay, fine. Just tell me this: how many Nordlings did you conjure up?"

The loon just shook his head.

"Don't you know?" Peggy insisted.

"Theoretically, there is an unlimited number of musical notes," Gavi replied. "Music is boundless, infinite; it is the underlying key to all universes."

"You're saying you have no idea how many? How did you keep track of them all?"

"He wouldn't let me give them names!" Molly burst out. "Oh, no. He decided we should *number* them. Can you believe that? Who ever heard of naming someone 'Re9'?"

"My star pupil!" Gavi wailed. "Please do not remind me. It is too painful!"

It was all Peggy could do to keep the two of them on track.

"All right, all right. You numbered them. But what do you mean they've disappeared? Where have they gone?"

"We cannot be certain," Gavi began. "But we suspect that —"

"We know where they are!" Molly interrupted him. "They're in the Hole at the Pole!"

Peggy burst out laughing. "The Hole at the Pole?"

"It's true! The Nobodaddy stole them!"

"The Nobodaddy!" exclaimed Peggy. "You're kidding, right? I mean, the Nobodaddy doesn't exist! We made him up as a joke!"

❖

"This is getting boring!" Molly complained.

They were playing their favourite game with the Nordlings, in which they pretended they were being chased by a swarm of invisible flesh-eating bugs called "NoSeeUms," like the ones Peggy had read about in Our Wondrous North.

Molly said she had a better idea.

"Let's pretend there's a really big monster chasing us! That'll make it more exciting!"

The Nordlings were thrilled by the idea, but Gavi was dubious.

"You have to be careful with pretending here in Notherland," he said.

"Why?" one of the littlest, Mi, piped up.

"Because everything here is pretend. Which means anything you pretend could become real."

"'Real'?" said Mi. "What does 'real' mean?"

"Oh!" the loon said, exasperated. "I do not know how to explain it to you!"

"Don't worry, Gavi," Molly reassured him. "We'll say it lives at the Pole! That's so far north, no monster could ever come all the way down here!"

"In a Hole at the Pole!" Peggy picked up on Molly's idea. "Because a hole is empty, there's nothing in it. See? It couldn't

become real!" She thought a moment. "I know! We'll call the monster 'Nobodaddy'!" She tripped over the word and quickly corrected herself.

"I mean 'Nobody'!"

But everyone was delighted with her mistake, especially the Nordlings. They loved saying the word over and over, giggling. And over time, the name stuck.

❖

I can't believe I'm doing this, Peggy thought as she walked through the woods behind the other two. She felt herself driven by some curious fascination as, one by one, each of her questions led to more questions.

If this is all a dream, I'll wake up soon, she thought. *I'll snap out of it and come to my senses. Or maybe I won't. Maybe I've gone completely crazy.*

Whichever it was, there seemed to be nothing else for her to do but stumble blindly ahead and see what happened next.

They found themselves standing by a large, fallen tree, and Molly pointed to its hollowed-out trunk. There, curled up in a ball, was a tiny creature, which Peggy recognized immediately as a Nordling.

She knelt down and gently touched the child's head.

"Which one are you?"

"This is Mi, the last remaining Nordling," Gavi said gravely. "We think the Nobodaddy does not realize he is missing one. At least we hope so. And we must keep him from discovering it."

The Nordling looked up at Peggy with wide, awe-struck eyes.

"Is it true?" she whispered.

"What?" Peggy asked.

"Are you really the Creator?"

Peggy looked at Gavi and Molly.

"I guess I am."

To Peggy's astonishment Mi fell upon her, clutching her around the waist.

"The others said they didn't believe in you, but not me! I knew you were real. I knew you'd come back one day!" She pulled away from Peggy and looked up at her pleadingly. "You'll bring back all the others, won't you? You'll make the RoryBory bright again. Won't you?"

✧

The Great Skyway came unfolding out of the sky, as it did every night, to transport the tired Nordlings up to their places along the great band of the RoryBory. There, each one was transformed into a column of pure, dancing light, sometimes white, other times tinged with pale green or pink or blue. They would spend the night in a sleeplike trance, immersed in a great swirling pool of light and sound, singing their musical notes and sending a glorious hum across the vast Northern sky.

Some nights the RoryBory was surrounded by darkness. Other times, like tonight, the whole sky was lit up, almost like day. A land where there is no darkness ...

Peggy was lying on her back looking up at the night sky. This was why she had created Notherland. No matter what happened back in her other life, here she felt safe.

"Does it seem to you that some nights the RoryBory is brighter than others?" she asked Molly.

Molly, tired out from playing, only murmured. But Gavi heard her and called over from where he was resting on the calm waters of the lake.

"Of course it is!"

"Why, Gavi?"

"It is perfectly simple. Elementary physics."

Molly began to let out a low groan, as if to say "There he goes again."

"Yeah?" said Peggy, silencing the doll with a light jab of her elbow.

"The RoryBory not only looks brighter," Gavi went on, "it is brighter. That is the nature of light. What it appears to be, it is. And light always becomes stronger in the presence of other light. 'Light increases light.' That is one of the basic laws of Notherland."

Peggy stifled a giggle. She knew Gavi was just making it all up. But she liked the sound of it: The Laws of Notherland.

"Gavi," she said, "you're a real philosopher."

"What's a philosopher?" Molly piped up, suddenly interested.

"A philosopher," Peggy replied, "is a person who thinks about things."

❖

It had grown dark, just as they'd said it would.

Peggy's mind was a jumble of images and sensations. She had just watched Mi make her way up the long sweep of the Great Skyway all by herself. Now, as Peggy lay down on some juniper boughs, she found it almost unbearably poignant to see that tiny point of light burning with such fierce intensity. It was as though the Nordling was determined to make up for her lost companions and light up the horizon by herself.

The enormity of what was happening finally began to sink in. She was really here, in Notherland, with her long-forgotten childhood companions. But how could that be? Why were these terrible things happening here? What would happen if the Nobodaddy ever caught Mi? Peggy knew that none of them wanted to speak their worst fear out loud: with no Nordlings left to light the night sky, would the whole world around them cease to exist?

But what could she do about it? Why had they summoned her here? If Notherland now existed on its own, as Gavi had said, then what happened here didn't have anything to do with her anymore. Did it?

She raised her head off the soft boughs and looked over at Molly. The doll's arms and legs jutted stiffly out from her body, and though she was lying down her eyes were wide open. *Dolls aren't like humans*, Peggy reminded herself. *They don't sleep.* She thought of how she used to tuck Molly under the covers with her, cradling the doll in her arms as she drifted off.

"Goodnight, Molly," she called softly.

"G'night, Peggy."

What am I doing? she chided herself. *I'm saying goodnight to a doll! This has got to be some kind of weird dream!*

Tomorrow morning, she told herself as she finally began to drift off, she'd wake up in her own bed. Or maybe she'd somehow passed out in Green Echo Park, in which case she'd come to any minute now. She'd pick herself up, get her flute case — which was certainly still lying there on the mound in the trees — and head back to that store ... the one with all the instruments ... what was it called?

CHAPTER 3

Above the Tree Line

PEGGY AWOKE THE NEXT MORNING to bright sun streaming through the branches of tall trees overhead.

I knew it, she thought. *I was here in the park all along!*

She squinted into the sunlight. The trees were awfully tall. Pines, they looked like.

My eyes are playing tricks on me.

She began to shake her head vigorously.

Maybe I fell and hit my head. Maybe that's how I passed out ...

The sound of a child's high-pitched laughter rang through the morning air. Peggy looked up. There was the Great Skyway, with Mi poised at the top.

Okay, fine, she thought. *If I'm not going to snap out of this, then I'll just have to figure out how to get myself home.*

There had to be a way. She resolved to talk with Gavi right away. Molly was stubborn, but Gavi would listen to reason. Peggy was sure she could make him understand why she had to leave. They'd managed to bring her here. Surely they'd know how to get her back.

The two of them were already up and about, waiting at the bottom of the Skyway for Mi to come down. Peggy watched the child as she glided effortlessly down the huge slide, giggling and squealing, and she remembered how all the Nordlings used to be so joyous and lighthearted. She marvelled that, in the midst of all the trouble, Mi could still be so apparently carefree.

Gavi noticed Peggy first.

"Good morning! How are you today?"

"Oh, I'm ..." At first, her voice trailed off uncertainly, then she decided she had to speak with firm resolve. "Gavi, I don't understand what's happening or how you brought me here, but I have to get back home. There are things I have to do. What's my mom going to think if I don't come home?"

"Oh, you need not worry about that," Gavi replied. "While you are here in Notherland, time in your other life is in suspension, so to speak. Your family and friends will not even know you are gone."

"So you're saying that for me, time has ... stopped?"

The loon nodded.

"Are you sure about that?"

"I cannot say with absolute certainty ..." he hesitated. "But it is my best guess!" he concluded brightly.

"And if your best guess is wrong?"

The loon looked at her thoughtfully.

"Yes, I see the problem. I must admit that when we brought you here, we did not consider the consequences for your life. We had only one thing in mind: how to save Notherland and the Nordlings. And we were hoping ..." he paused a moment before continuing, "that you would know."

"Know what?"

"How to save Notherland."

"Me?" said Peggy.

"You are the Creator."

"You said yourself that Notherland isn't under my control anymore."

"I said it *appeared* to have grown beyond your control. For all we know, that is because you have been away so long. You have forgotten what you used to know. There was a time when everything in Notherland flowed from you. You might still have some powers here. Maybe now that you have remembered us, now that you are actually back in Notherland ..."

"Gavi ..." For a moment Peggy was at a loss for words. "I'd like to help you. I really would. But I don't belong here. I'm not a little kid anymore."

"See?" Molly shouted. "What'd I tell you? She's stopped caring about us. Either that, or she's a coward!"

"Stop it, Molly," Gavi scolded her. "We brought Peggy back here. If she is to stay and help us, it has to be her own free choice."

✧

As the four of them made their way back to Painted Rock, Peggy trailed behind, relieved that she didn't have to look at their faces. Mi, especially, was having a hard time, fighting back tears the whole way. It made Peggy feel rotten, as though she was abandoning them. And it didn't help all that much that Gavi was being so understanding about everything. In truth, Peggy found Molly's anger easier to deal with.

They arrived back at Lake Notherland and walked along the shore to the smooth rock face. Peggy stared at it for a moment.

"You're sure this is the one?" she said to Gavi.

"Oh, yes," he replied. "This is Painted Rock."

He must be right, she figured. The face of the rock was covered here and there with reddish-brown markings of various shapes and sizes. But other than that, it was indistinguishable from the other large rocks that lined that part of Lake Notherland's shoreline.

"Okay. Just how did I used to do this?" she asked.

"You just ..." Gavi searched for the word, "did it. That is, I never really understood how you did it. You just stood in front of the rock and somehow, it happened. You would pass through to the other side."

"Okay," she said, taking a deep breath. "Let's see what happens."

Now there was no avoiding it. She had to face them. It was time to say goodbye.

Molly kept her eyes down. Her expression was hard and unyielding. But Gavi looked warmly into Peggy's eyes.

"Goodbye, Peggy. It has meant so much to see you again. Please do not feel bad about your decision. We understand why you must go back."

Peggy choked back a tear.

"Thanks, Gavi. It's meant a lot to me, too."

She turned to say goodbye to Mi. But the little Nordling turned away with a wrenching sob and buried her face in Gavi's feathers.

I feel like a total rat, Peggy thought.

She stood in front of Painted Rock and closed her eyes, trying to remember what it used to be like when she was little. She had a vague memory of the surface of the rock growing transparent, as though she could look right through it and see Green Echo Park on the other side. But after a few moments, when she opened her eyes, Painted Rock looked as solid and impenetrable as it had a moment before.

She turned away and closed her eyes again. But now, all she could see in her mind's eye was Mi's face, contorted in agony.

Great, she thought ruefully. *That sure makes it easier.*

She tried to concentrate on the rock. But no matter how hard she tried she couldn't push Mi's face out of her mind.

"I can't do this!" she burst out.

"You mean it is not working?" Gavi asked.

"I keep thinking I remember how to do it, but it slips away from me." She turned to them. "What am I going to do?"

"It is possible that you are trying too hard," Gavi suggested in a helpful tone. "Perhaps in a little while your powers, and your memory of how to use them, will come back to you."

Hearing Gavi's words, Peggy felt a momentary panic: *What if they don't come back?* But she firmly pushed the thought aside. It was ridiculous to think she might be trapped here. Things would set themselves right soon. Somehow.

"Okay, maybe it'll come back to me later, but when?" she finally said aloud. "And what am I supposed to do in the meantime?"

"Well, you can sit and whine about it," Molly said, her voice dripping with sarcasm. "Or you can make yourself useful and try to help us."

They all looked at Peggy. No one spoke for a few moments.

"Fine," she sighed. "But I'll only stay till I figure out how to get myself back home. Understand?"

Molly looked at Peggy with a look of wary surprise, and Mi bounded over and threw her arms around her.

"O thank you! Thank you, Pay-gee!" she said earnestly. "This morning was the first time I did not wake up frightened. I was so happy, because our Creator had come back to us."

"Whoa, sweetie, it's only for a little while," Peggy said, hugging Mi back. But she knew the little Nordling was barely listening now.

As she stroked the child's head fondly, she thought of her flute case. Was it still there in the park? Someone had surely found it sitting there on the ground by now. Maybe they were walking into Around Again that very minute, exchanging it for the money that should have been hers.

Great, she thought. *What have I gotten myself into now?*

✧

"You're going *where?*"

"You heard me," Molly replied. "If the Nobodaddy's keeping the Nordlings as prisoners at the Hole at the Pole, we have to go there."

"But ..." Peggy sputtered, "you've never *been* to the Hole at the Pole. You don't even know how to find it."

Molly rolled her single eye in disgust.

"My best guess," said Gavi softly, "would be to go North. What do you think?"

"Yeah, I guess that's fairly obvious," Peggy admitted sheepishly. "But say you do find the Pole. What are you going to do when you get there?"

"Free the Nordlings, silly!" Molly cried.

"I know, but how?" Peggy shot back.

Gavi gave her a penetrating look and sighed.

"To be quite honest ... we have no idea."

Peggy looked at the three of them. Here they were, preparing to set off into uncharted territory to fight an unknown enemy, armed with nothing but Molly's bravado, Gavi's theories and Mi's loving, implicit trust in them both. What a crew.

She stood up slowly.

"Okay, let's get started."

"What?" Molly gasped. "You're coming with us?"

Peggy nodded.

"Hurray!" Mi cheered. "You are the one who can bring the Nordlings back and make the RoryBory bright again. I know you are!"

"But I thought you planned to stay here, close to Painted Rock, so you could try again to return to your world," Gavi said.

Peggy shrugged. "What am I going to do? Sit around twiddling my thumbs while you go off to fight the Nobodaddy? Anyway, if you don't mind my saying so, I think you folks could use a bit of help."

"That," Molly said impatiently, "is exactly what we've been trying to tell you since you got here!"

Peggy smiled grimly, and they set about making their plans for the long journey. None of them had ever explored the farthest reaches of Notherland, and they weren't at all sure how long they might have to travel. One of the first things they realized was that someone would have to carry Mi, who couldn't walk fast enough to keep up.

"I could easily carry Mi on my back on water," said Gavi, "but I am too awkward to help her on land."

"I think I've got just the solution," Peggy said, and she set about tearing a couple of small leg-holes in the bottom of her knapsack, adapting it into a carrier. She lifted Mi into it and swung it up onto her back.

"Whee!" cried the child.

"There's something I've been meaning to ask you," Peggy said as they set off. "How is it that Mi has escaped the Nobodaddy all this time?"

"He doesn't know!" Molly laughed. "He thinks he's got them all."

Gavi explained, "There is only one way he could tell for sure that he does not have all the Nordlings, and that would be if he noticed that one of the notes in the musical scale was missing."

"But he won't!" Molly piped up.

"Why?" Peggy demanded.

"Because the Nobodaddy is such a coarse, primitive being," replied Gavi, "I believe he has no 'ear for music,' as you humans put it. In fact, he does not hear it as music at all, the way we do, but as a horrible, grating noise. Therefore the musical scale means nothing to him. He cannot tell one tone from another."

"So as long as Mi doesn't sing, there's no way he can tell she's missing!" Molly concluded.

Peggy shook her head. These two never lacked explanations for things they knew nothing about. "You're just making all this up as you go along!" she said in exasperation.

"As you did with Notherland itself!" Gavi replied pointedly. "I know what you must think about all this, but I assure you I have given these matters a great deal of careful thought. In fact, thinking is what I do almost all of the time, and I have concluded that the Nobodaddy's interest in the Nordlings has nothing to do with their musicality. He steals them for their light only."

"Light?" The drift of Gavi's theories was starting to make a bit more sense. "Why would he want their light?"

"Because the Hole at the Pole is similar to what some in your world call a Black Hole. A place of endless darkness from which light, once swallowed up, cannot escape. At the Pole, a reversal of the magnetic field occurs, and strange things happen that defy normal laws — not only of your world, but those of Notherland, too. It makes sense that the Nobodaddy would live in such a place, because he is a creature who represents the opposite of everything Notherland was created for. It is a world of light, yet he lives in darkness. It is a world of safety, yet he brings danger."

"That still doesn't explain why he'd steal the Nordlings," Peggy said.

"Who knows?" Gavi replied with a sigh, because at times even he got tired of thinking so much. "Perhaps the endless darkness he lives in is intolerable to him. Perhaps stealing the Nordlings is his misguided attempt to bring light into the Hole at the Pole. In any case, we will find out soon enough if things are as I say."

With all this talk, it suddenly dawned on Peggy that her stomach was rumbling.

"Can we stop for a minute? I'm starving."

"Starving? Oh, my good heavens!" Gavi exclaimed.

"Whoa, Gavi, don't take me so literally. It's just a way of saying I'm hungry."

"Hmm." Gavi stopped to ponder. "Another problem I failed to anticipate. Eating is something the three of us do not have to think about."

"Maybe you can stop and catch her a fish at the next lake," Molly suggested.

"Mmm, fish. That sounds good!" Peggy perked up, but Gavi shook his head.

"I have never gotten very good at things like fishing. Since I am not a flesh-and-blood loon, I have no need to eat, and do not bother to catch fish for myself."

"Come on, there must be something in Notherland I can eat." Peggy looked around. "Something easy, like blueberries."

Gavi and Molly look at one another quizzically.

"Blueberries?"

"What are those?"

"You mean," said Peggy, "all that time I spent here when I was little and we never came across any blueberry bushes?"

The two of them shook their heads.

"Ohhh," she groaned. "Thinking about it is driving me crazy. What I wouldn't give for a handful of plump, juicy, ripe blueberries right now."

"You mean like those?" Molly pointed to some low bushes. A few yards away from where they stood, dark-blue berries were hanging in clusters so heavy they dragged the branches right down to the ground.

"Yeah!" Peggy cried, and she immediately set to picking them. The others watched, fascinated, as she gorged on great handfuls of berries like a ravenous bear cub.

Between mouthfuls, she tried to speak.

"Thwahemmmmmm!"

"What?" Molly said.

"They were right here! I must've seen them out of the corner of my eye! That's what made me think of blueberries."

"We did not see them," Gavi pointed out.

"Of course you didn't! You didn't even know what blueberries were until a minute ago!"

"Then again," Gavi went on thoughtfully, "maybe you *made* them appear."

Peggy looked at the loon. "What do you mean?"

"It is possible that by thinking so hard about blueberries, you conjured them up."

"Like I did when I was little? You really think so?"

"Did she dream the berries to life?" Mi asked excitedly.

"Possibly," Gavi said. "If so, it might be a sign that your imagination still exerts power in Notherland."

The loon looked at her, and Peggy knew he was thinking

the same thing she was. If she made the berries appear, did that mean she could make Painted Rock open up? Could she go home now? Should she go back and try?

Then again, what if Gavi was wrong? Maybe the blueberries were there all along, and she just hadn't noticed them. Maybe she'd go back to Painted Rock and nothing would happen. Then she'd be stuck there by herself while the other three went on to the Pole without her. Maybe it was better to wait and find out for sure if her imaginative powers were coming back. And if they were ...

Finally Gavi spoke up.

"If you wish to go back to Painted Rock, we will understand."

Peggy just shook her head and started walking.

❖

They had been walking through dense woods, but now they abruptly found themselves standing at the edge of a vast stretch of treeless tundra.

"What happened?" Peggy asked.

"Have you forgotten *everything*?" said Molly impatiently. "It's the Tree Line, silly!"

The Tree Line. Peggy remembered seeing the term in *Our Wondrous North*. The book had never explained exactly what it meant, and she assumed that somewhere in the North was an actual "line" of trees. Now, of course, she understood that the Tree Line was actually a zone between the Northern woods and the tundra where the trees gradually become stunted and sparse, and finally disappear altogether. But here,

Peggy saw what she had long ago pictured in her mind's eye: a final row of magnificently tall pines stretching each way as far as the eye could see.

It was getting late in the day. Peggy and Molly sat down by a stream as Gavi took a swim to refresh himself. Mi went along the bank, picking up stones. Everywhere they stopped, the Nordling would scavenge for what she proudly called "treasure." *Just like any little kid*, Peggy thought to herself.

Mi ran over to show off her latest find.

"Look!"

It was a stubby hollow tube with a couple of holes in it. Peggy looked it over.

"What do you think it is?"

"Not sure," Peggy shrugged. "Maybe a bone."

"What kind? From an animal?"

"Probably," Peggy smiled.

"I'm going to keep it!" Mi clutched it as she scampered back over to the stream. As they sat watching her, Peggy turned to Molly.

"How can you be so brave, Molly? Aren't you even a little bit scared?"

Molly shook her head. "The Nobodaddy doesn't scare me. I'm not made of light, like the Nordlings. I don't have anything he'd be interested in stealing."

"But he's destroying your world. What if we can't figure out how to stop him?"

"I don't think about those things!" Molly said defiantly. "Anyway, at least this is an adventure. Which is more than I ever had with you."

"What do you mean?" Peggy was taken aback by the accusing tone in Molly's voice.

"You used to leave me for days at a time, lying in a heap of toys on your bed!"

Peggy was flabbergasted. "But Molly ... that's what kids *do* with dolls."

"That's the trouble!" Molly snapped. "I was happy enough just being a doll, until you gave me this stupid eyepatch. You went on and on about how it made me look just like a pirate, about how pirates were brave and had adventures. You put all these ideas into my head. But you didn't give me any of the things a pirate *needs* to be a pirate. Like a ship! And a sea to sail it on! And a sword!"

"Molly, I'm sorry. I never knew you felt that way ... I was only trying to make you feel better. After you ..." her voice trailed off awkwardly.

"After I lost my eye? Sure, I knew that's what you were trying to do. And it worked. It did make me feel better. I started to think of myself as this daring, adventurous pirate roaming the high seas. But then you left us. All of a sudden, you just stopped coming here. So now I have to settle for riding around on Gavi's back on Lake Notherland, the puniest excuse for an ocean there ever was! And for a sword, I have to use a fallen tree branch! That's why I'm not scared of the Nobodaddy, or anything else. Don't tell Gavi I said this, but secretly I'm glad that all this has happened. I've been waiting my whole life to make this journey! My destiny awaits me at the Hole at the Pole! I just know it!"

Molly abruptly fell silent. She wasn't accustomed to talking for such long stretches. For a few moments the two of them just sat quietly.

Peggy was lost in thought, wishing she felt as courageous and ready for adventure as Molly.

Suddenly she looked around. "What's that?"

Molly listened, puzzled.

"What?"

"I hear something," Peggy said. "Some kind of low drone."

"What's a drone?"

"Like a buzz or a hum," Peggy continued. "It's getting louder. Almost like a swarm of bugs."

"Bugs?" There was alarm in Molly's voice.

"Don't you hear it now?"

Suddenly Gavi shouted over to them.

"Molly! Peggy!"

Peggy turned to see Gavi lunge toward Mi and attempt to shield her with his large black wing.

"What's going on?"

"It's the nozeems!"

"Huh?"

Peggy couldn't make out what he was saying. She turned to Molly, who started screaming too.

"Run, Peggy! Nozeems!"

Peggy turned back and watched in horror as Gavi began to writhe and bat the air around him, even as he kept Mi covered with one wing. Had they both gone completely crazy?

The buzzing sound grew louder and louder, till it seemed to be hovering right above her head. Then she remembered:

the game she used to play with the Nordlings, pretending that they were being attacked by swarms of tiny, flesh-eating bugs.

NoSeeUms!

So that was what Molly and Gavi were saying!

At first they just seemed to buzz around her. But soon she began to feel tiny sharp pinpricks all over her skin. She looked over at Gavi. The swarm was encircling him, and it would be only a matter of moments before they managed to get in underneath his wing and start feasting on Mi.

For a few moments Peggy batted uselessly at the air, shouting furiously, "Go on! Get away!" Then a thought siezed her: why not try *imagining* them away?

Maybe all those powers that came so easily to her as a little girl really were coming back! Notherland was her place, the product of *her* imagination. She was the Creator! It was time to start acting like it!

As swarms of NoSeeUms buzzed around her, she focussed her mind, trying to imagine them dispersing, flying away, just as vividly as she had relished the thought of eating blueberries earlier.

Imagine, she told herself. *Believe!*

She felt an unbearable tickling as some of the NoSeeUms burrowed into her ears and hair.

Think!

Now they were making their way up into her nose!

Think harder!

"What's the matter with you?"

She opened her eyes to see Molly, thrusting Mi at her, yelling, "Snap out of it! Take her and follow me!"

"Where?"

"Anywhere! Now get moving! Run!"

And Peggy did exactly as she was told.

Chapter 4

Jackpine

How they managed to outrun the NoSeeUms, Peggy wasn't sure. All she knew was that, having run almost to the limit of her endurance, she stopped and realized, with enormous relief, that the swarms of bugs were no longer following them. Instead of the low drone of their incessant buzzing, there was silence.

At least I managed to keep Mi from getting eaten alive, Peggy thought as she sat scratching at the bites.

"Another few moments and I would have been nothing but a pile of bones and gristle!" Gavi declared with high drama, rolling around on his back in a vain attempt to relieve the nagging itch. After Molly had scooped Mi out from under his wing and scurried away with her, Gavi had managed to get away from the NoSeeUms by diving into the middle of the stream, where the water was just deep enough to cover his body.

Peggy looked over at Molly, who was sitting comfortably a few feet away. *Not a bite on her!* Peggy thought enviously. Being a doll had its advantages.

"If only," Gavi went on, moaning, "you had thought to

try imagining them away!"

"I did," she replied sourly.

"What?"

"I tried imagining them away."

"Oh."

"Some Creator, eh?"

Gavi thought a moment.

"Perhaps, like everything here, your powers have undergone changes and are of a different order than when you were younger. It might take some time before you rediscover how to use them."

Molly called over to them. She was pointing to something in the distance.

"Look. Is that a tree?"

"It couldn't be," said Peggy. "Not here."

"Then what is it?"

"Let's go see," Peggy replied. Anything to get her mind off the insane itching!

As they got closer, it became clear that it was, indeed, a tree.

"A jack pine," Gavi said. "To be precise."

"But what would a jack pine be doing so far above the Tree Line?" Peggy asked, walking up to it and fingering one of its branches.

"Well," Gavi speculated, "the jack pine is a very hardy species. A seed, perhaps even a whole pine cone, could have gotten blown this far by the wind —"

"What was that?"

"Molly," Gavi sighed, "must you *always* interrupt people

when they are speaking?"

"But I heard something. It sounded like a voice."

"But we're the only ones here," Peggy pointed out. She turned back to Gavi. "Even if a seed could have travelled this far, how could it have grown? It's so barren here." She absent-mindedly touched the branch again.

"I know it seems unlikely, but it is the only explanation I can ..." Gavi was distracted by Mi tugging at one of his wings.

"I hear something, too," she said in her sweet, high voice.

"I heard it again! When you touched the branch!" Molly blurted out.

Peggy looked at Gavi. "Did you hear anything?"

"I might have heard something, but —"

"Touch the tree again!" Molly commanded.

"Why?"

"Just see what happens!"

Peggy reached over and touched the needles of one branch.

"Yessss!"

She looked around. This time she had distinctly heard something, too.

"A talking tree? Of course. Why should I be surprised?"

"I'm *not* a tree!"

They all gasped. It was unmistakable this time. It was a voice, and it was coming from the jack pine.

"Don't pull away!" the voice said urgently. "Touch me again."

They all looked at one another.

"Please. It's my only chance!"

Peggy hesitantly reached over and touched the branch once more.

"Hold on this time. Please! Don't let go!"

Almost involuntarily, she tightened her grip. As she held on, they all stood, gaping in amazement, and watched the tree become transparent, its branches fading into pale wisps, as the outline of a solid form appeared to emerge from it. After a few moments, Peggy realized with a shock that it was not a branch she was holding onto but a human hand.

The jack pine had disappeared completely. In its place stood a young man.

✧

For the longest time, Peggy couldn't take her eyes off him. Who was he? Where did he come from? How did he come to be here in Notherland? And most unnerving of all, why did he look vaguely familiar? She had the nagging sense that she'd seen him somewhere before.

At first he stood stock-still, his feet rooted to the ground, his legs straight like a tree trunk, his arms stretched outward, like pine branches. His eyes were the first to move, shifting back and forth warily. He turned his head side to side, slowly lifted one foot off the ground, then the other. Realizing that his arms were no longer encased in branches, he began to move them, wiggling his fingers in front of his face with a look of utter amazement. Then he began touching his face again and again, as if to assure himself that he was really there. At first his movements were stiff, like Molly's, but gradually they became easier, more fluid.

Finally he jumped into the air and let out a whoop. "WHOOEE!"

The others were startled, but Mi laughed with a sweet, bubbling lilt. The young man looked around, agitated.

"What was that?"

"It's just Mi," Molly said, pointing to the little creature peering out from inside the knapsack.

"That voice ... it's just like the others ..."

Gavi sprang towards him. "Others? What others?"

"Never mind," the young man said.

"Have you heard others like her?" the loon persisted. "Where? You must tell us."

"I don't want to talk about it!" the young man said angrily. He turned away.

Gavi and Peggy looked at one another, uncertain whether to press him further. Gavi spoke softly.

"Perhaps I should explain why we want to know. You see, we are on our way to the Hole at the Pole because we think that the Nobodaddy might have —"

"The Nobodaddy?" The young man turned on Gavi with a dark look. He suddenly grabbed the loon by the neck.

"What about the Nobodaddy? Did he send you after me? Is that why you're here? To do his dirty work?"

Gavi let loose with a high, fearful tremolo. Molly pounded the young man angrily on the back and Peggy grabbed his arm. "Leave him alone! What's the matter with you?"

"If you're with the Nobodaddy, I swear I'll kill you right now!"

"He's not with the Nobodaddy! None of us are! We're on our way to the Pole to stop him!"

The young man let go and looked at them long and hard, breathing heavily. Peggy could see how much effort it took for him to contain his rage.

"Sorry," he finally said. "Just hearing that name after all this time ..."

"Maybe you'd better begin at the beginning," Peggy said. "Just who are you?"

The young man looked her right in the eye.

"I have no idea," he replied.

✧

The young man's story was so fragmented, and he became so agitated while telling it, that it was a while before they could make much sense of it. But the source of his fierce hatred for the Nobodaddy quickly became clear. According to the young man, the Nobodaddy had robbed him of his most precious possession.

"I look like I'm standing right here before you, don't I? But I'm not. Part of me, the part that knows who I am, that has a name and a life and a memory — that part of me is off in another world somewhere."

"Then what are you doing here?" Peggy asked.

"That's what I'm trying to tell you!" he shot back impatiently. "I'm a Soul."

"A Soul?"

"The Nobodaddy stole me. That's what he does. He steals Souls!"

"You mean there are more like you?" Gavi asked.

"Are you kidding?" the young man said with a bitter laugh. "The Hole at the Pole is filled with more Souls than you can count!"

"But what about her?" Gavi pointed to Mi. "You said there were other beings like her at the Pole, too."

The young man nodded gravely.

"The little ones who sing? Oh, they're there all right. And they sure must have something special, because the Nobodaddy keeps them way down in the deepest part of the Hole. The rest of us could hear them from time to time. I swear, hearing those little voices was all that kept me going sometimes."

"But how does he keep them all as prisoners down there?"

"That's the mysterious thing. The Hole exerts some kind of powerful inward pull that traps you and keeps pulling you down, no matter how hard you fight it."

"Then how did you get out?" Peggy asked.

"He let me go. I was always stirring up the other Souls. I'd try to convince them we should stand up to him. There were so many of us, and only one of him. I thought if we all pulled together we could find a way to get free. But the people in the Hole are so frustrating! Once they've been down there a while it's like they just give up. They don't believe they can ever be free, so they stop trying.

"Then, one time I was on the ledge of the Hole, right near the outer rim, and just for a moment I could feel the inward pull of the Hole easing up. I quickly slipped out over the edge and yelled to the others around me to come, too. But they wouldn't. They were just too afraid. I couldn't believe it! They could've made a break for it, and they all just froze!

"Then the Hole started to pull in again. They all began shouting at me. 'Go! Get away! We can't get free, but at least you can!'

"So I made a mad dash for the open water that surrounds the Hole and jumped in. I swam for I don't know how long. The water was on the edge of freezing and I didn't know how long I could last. Somehow I kept going, till I got to the big ice field on the other side and started running again. When I got to the tundra I suddenly just stopped. I realized I had no idea who I was or where I was going or how to find my way back to the life I had before. I was free, but ..."

"But what?"

"I played right into his hands!" he spat out bitterly. "The Nobodaddy had deliberately let me go. I was a troublemaker and he wanted to get rid of me. He knew I'd get completely lost or die trying to escape. So it didn't matter that I was free, because either way, he'd won. I was so angry, I grabbed what I thought was a rock and started pounding the tundra with it. But it wasn't a rock, it was a pine cone. The ground was so hard the cone exploded and a shower of seeds came shooting out. They seemed to surround me like a mist, which grew thicker and thicker, until finally I realized it was wood. A tree, a full-grown jack pine, had instantly taken root right on this spot, and I was trapped inside it.

"I have no idea how long I was in there — days, months, years? I was in this slowed-down kind of half-awake state. It wasn't until you came along that I started to come out of it.

The instant you touched me," he turned to Peggy, "it was like I was jolted awake. My voice came back, I could feel my body again. But then you pulled your hand away and I could feel myself falling back into a stupor. That's why I had to make you hold on," he said, grabbing her hand, "to give me time to fight my way out of the tree." He dropped her hand again, suddenly embarrassed.

"My worst fear has come true!" Gavi burst out.

They all looked at him.

"What's wrong?" Peggy asked.

"Just as Notherland has taken on a life of its own, so has the Nobodaddy. Just as Notherland has gone beyond its boundaries, so has he."

"Stop talking in riddles!" Molly said impatiently.

Gavi burst out with a long wail.

"How could I have made such a terrible mistake? How could I have done this to my Creator?" He turned to Peggy. "We should never have brought you here! The Nobodaddy is not just abducting Nordlings. He is stalking the world on the other side of Painted Rock, stealing Souls from there! We thought you were the one who could save us, but now I see that we have put you in grave danger!"

The young man broke in.

"He's right. They haven't got souls," he said, pointing to Gavi and Molly, "but you do. You're a sitting duck for the Nobodaddy. If you're smart, you'll get out of here as fast as you can."

Gavi agreed. "You must go straight back to Painted Rock! Immediately!"

"We don't want him to get you, too!" Mi cried.

"But I can't leave now!" Peggy objected. "I don't even know if I can figure out how to get back."

"You must try. At least you will have a chance of saving yourself."

"I thought saving Notherland depended on me. That's why you brought me here!"

"We were wrong to do so. I did not realize the danger we were putting you into," Gavi replied.

"What about going up to the Pole?"

"We will go."

"By yourselves? No!" Peggy said. "I can't let you do that!"

"There is no other choice," Gavi insisted. "You must go back to Painted Rock for your own safety."

The young man stepped forward.

"Don't worry about them," he said firmly. "I'll go with them."

They all looked at him, astonished.

"You? Back to the Pole?"

"How can you think of it?"

"So I can get back at him for what he did to me," the young man said fiercely. "Nothing would give me greater satisfaction than to kick the Nobodaddy so far down that Hole he'll never find his way out again."

"Wait a minute," Peggy said firmly. "If you try to go back there, you'll be in even more danger than I am. What do you think the Nobodaddy's going to do with you once he finds out you're still alive? You should come back to Painted Rock with me. I'll try to figure out how to get us both back."

The young man shook his head. "Forget it. Why should I go back there? I don't know if I'm ever going to find out who I am again. Anyway, I won't be able to live with myself unless I do what I can to free the others in there."

"So let's do it!" shouted Molly, who had been growing more and more restless during the whole exchange. "Let's get going!"

Peggy stood listening as they began to make plans, all talking excitedly at once. It had been bad enough when she thought her worst problem was not being able to get back home. Now it was starting to sink in that there might be real danger for her here. Clearly, there were things going on in Notherland that none of them, even Gavi, fully understood. This young man didn't belong in "her" Notherland, but here he was. And his warning ... What if her soul was stolen? What if she got trapped down in the Hole like the others?

Gavi was right, of course. The sensible thing to do was to go to Painted Rock. Maybe she just needed to keep at it. Maybe if she'd kept trying long enough her powers would have driven back the NoSeeUms. There was certainly no point sticking around here. She'd done all she could to help. Notherland would go on without her. It was time to go back to her own life ...

Molly was speaking.

"You can carry Mi for us!"

"Sure, no problem," the young man replied.

"He can use Peggy's knapsack!" the doll exclaimed. "It's perfect."

They're talking about me like I'm already gone! Peggy thought.

Gavi, as if sensing her dismay, looked at Peggy. "Will you be all right?" he asked. "Can you find your way back on your own?"

"Sure, I'll be okay," Peggy replied.

She slid the pack off her back but stood holding it for a moment.

"Hold on a sec. Why should I go back now? You said the Nobodaddy doesn't know about Mi. He doesn't know I'm here either."

"You cannot take the risk!" Gavi objected.

"How's he going to find out?" Peggy insisted. "I've come this far. I don't want to go back. I created this place, and if anybody's going to save it ..." she said, taking a slow, deep breath, "it's going to be me!"

❖

As they prepared to set off, Peggy scooped up the knapsack with Mi in it.

"Let me take that," the young man offered.

"It's okay ..." Peggy protested, but he hoisted the pack onto his back anyway and began walking.

Peggy caught up to him.

"Why don't we take turns?"

"Okay."

"What's your name?" Mi asked the young man brightly as they walked along.

He shook his head. "Don't have one."

"No name!" she exclaimed. "Everyone's got a name!"

"I must've had one before. I just don't remember it."

"Tell you what!" said Mi. "I'll think of a name for you until you remember your real one!"

"It's a deal."

She considered a moment. Since he was not a Nordling, she decided it should be a name with two sounds. Suddenly her head snapped up.

"I know! How about 'Jackpine'?"

They looked at the young man to see his reaction. He squinted thoughtfully for a moment.

"In a way, I owe my life to that tree. It kept me hidden all that time," he said. "Sure, why not? Jackpine it is."

"Jackpine! Jackpine!" Heartily pleased with herself, Mi kept chirping the name.

Peggy wasn't sure how she felt about having this stranger along. His presence added a new, unstable element to the journey. Still, as she watched him walking, bouncing Mi in the knapsack, she had to admit that it was refreshing to have another person around, someone her own age, someone with a recognizably human face and body ...

Her thoughts were interrupted by a familiar loon call.

"Look!" Gavi cried.

Up ahead of them was a vast, smooth, seemingly endless sheet of unbroken ice.

❖

"Now I know why they call it Everlasting. It goes on forever and ever!" Molly said peevishly.

"Actually," Gavi pointed out, "the word 'everlasting' refers not to the distance but to the fact that the ice never melts."

Peggy smiled to herself. Neither of them knew that "Everlasting Ice" was a term the Arctic explorers had used for the polar ice cap. She'd found it in *Our Wondrous North* and borrowed it for Notherland because she loved the sound of it. And instead of the craggy white terrain the explorers had found, she'd imagined the Everlasting Ice as a great glassy skating rink. Now, here she was, laying eyes on it for the first time.

As they gazed out over the huge ice field, another uncomfortable fact was becoming evident: it was getting colder. They were fine in the daylight, while the sun still warmed the air. But if they started their crossing now, what would they do come nightfall? Neither Gavi, with his feathers, nor the plastic Molly would be bothered by the cold, and Mi, of course, would spend the night in the RoryBory. But Jackpine and Peggy would have to find some way to shelter themselves while they slept.

Jackpine's proposal was to get across the ice as quickly as possible, to reach the open sea surrounding the Pole.

Molly thought this was ridiculous.

"How can there be open water up there?" she challenged him.

"There is. I swam across it."

"But it's even colder than here!"

"No, it's warmer. I swear it is!"

"That makes no sense!" Molly said firmly, turning to Gavi for confirmation. "Does it?"

"No," he replied. "But then again, we are encountering many things that do not make sense."

"Maybe it's like you said — the Nobodaddy is the opposite of everything that's true in Notherland. So as we get nearer the Pole, more opposite things are going to happen," Peggy offered.

"That could be," Gavi agreed. "But then we will have a whole new problem on our hands: how to get across the open water. It will be no problem for me, of course. And if Jackpine was able to swim across it before —"

"But I can't swim!" Molly burst out. "What do I do?"

Gavi assured her they would come up with a solution, but there wasn't a lot of conviction in his voice.

Jackpine was getting impatient.

"Let's figure it out when we get there! I don't know about the rest of you, but I don't want to turn into an icicle while I sleep."

He strode purposefully out onto the Everlasting Ice and began to propel himself across it, alternately running and sliding. The others followed him, moving more gingerly. The ice was very slick, and at first they just skidded around, pitching sideways and backwards, sometimes tumbling down. Their progress was frustratingly slow, and soon Jackpine was well ahead of them, with Mi in the knapsack.

"How does he do that?" Molly asked.

"He's had a chance to get used to it," Peggy replied, watching his taut, wiry body as he glided across the icy surface. "He almost looks like he's skating. That's what we have to do!"

"What?"

"Pretend we're on skates!" she said with conviction.

"What are skates?" Molly asked.

Gavi began to launch into one of his elaborate explanations of a human invention. "It is a pair of metal blades, worn on the bottom of the feet in order to —"

"Just watch me," Peggy broke in. "Both of you. Watch the way I move."

She began to shift from foot to foot, pushing herself forward with a smooth gliding motion.

Molly tried. At first it felt awkward. For a doll, this kind of fluid movement didn't come easily. But gradually she began to get the hang of it. She limbered up and zipped away as fast as she could, bolting far ahead of the others. The sound of her laughter rang through the crisp, cold air.

"Wheeeee!"

Gavi decided that he would prefer to fly, which surprised them. He wasn't very good at it, so he flew only rarely.

They realized he'd need help taking off, since loons normally need to skitter over a long expanse of water in order to work up enough speed. They decided to race ahead of him, pulling him along the ice atop Peggy's jacket while he flapped his wings enough to get airborne.

"This is fun!" Molly shouted as they whizzed along. Peggy pulled one sleeve of the jacket, Jackpine the other. They watched the loon hover, his wings whirring rapidly. Then he began skimming along the surface of the ice.

"Yippee!" Mi cried as Gavi finally soared into the air above them.

Now they all felt as though they were flying. Peggy suggested they form a chain and play crack-the-whip. As her fingers curved around Jackpine's, she felt a buzz of excitement, almost like an electric current, run through her body.

Suddenly they heard a tremolo call above their heads.

"Gavi? Is something wrong?"

"I don't know," he called down. "I see something on the ice up ahead of us."

"What is it?" Jackpine asked.

"I'm not sure," Gavi replied hesitantly. "It looks like some kind of ... ship."

Molly whirled around and looked up at him.

"Ship?" she yelled. "Did you say *ship?*" And she took off in a mad dash across the Everlasting Ice.

CHAPTER 5

Lord and Lady

SIR JOHN SURVEYED THE VAST EXPANSE of ice with his spyglass, as he was accustomed to doing several times a day.

"My dear!" his wife, Lady Jane, called to him. "Your tea is getting cold."

At the mention of tea, Sir John collapsed the spyglass and crossed the deck to join her. She handed him a small plate, slightly cracked with a faded blue flower design, bearing a crumpet with Devon cream. He took it from her eagerly.

"Ah, yes," he said. "I will certainly have one of these." He dipped it in the cream and took a bite. "Mmm. Delicious. However do you do it, my dear?"

"As I always say, Sir John, a true lady knows how to make the best of her circumstances. You have been gazing out on the ice more than usual today, my dear. Are you feeling all right? Is your gout acting up again?"

"No, no. I feel in the best of health. It's just that ..."

"Yes?"

"The past while, I swear I could hear ... sounds in the distance."

"The usual cracks and shifts, no doubt. You know how

the ice seems more restless some days than others."

"No, my dear. This is different. Almost like ... voices. Oh, but I know that's preposterous, though sometimes I ..." Sir John voice trailed off.

"What, dear?"

"Sometimes I wonder if I am going mad out here."

"You mustn't talk that way, Sir John. Everyone faces difficulties in life. But we must have faith that things will turn out for the best."

Lady Jane picked up her embroidery hoop as Sir John sipped his tea and fell silent. He did not want to distress his beloved Jane with this cockeyed talk of voices out on the ice. Indeed, he believed he would undoubtedly have gone mad long ago were it not for the calming influence of his beloved Jane. Jane, who had steadfastly believed in him through so many years of this Arctic imprisonment. Jane, who had commissioned search party after search party, refusing to believe what the rest of England maintained: that all hope was lost, that her husband and the gallant crews of both his ships, the *Erebus* and the *Terror*, were all dead. Jane, who had one day suddenly, miraculously, appeared here on the vast Arctic ice, ending his long, lonely vigil. At first he'd been unable to believe his own eyes and thought that he, too, had finally followed his crewmen into Eternity. But no, here he was, still on the *Terror*, with his wife, as ever a vision of comely womanliness, her smile radiating warmth and love.

And so they had settled into life together on the ship, keeping to a routine of daily walks on the ice and afternoon tea — mysteriously, the ship's stores had not been exhausted.

Sir John, out of delicacy, did not inquire how Lady Jane had managed to make her way, apparently alone, to this remote part of the Arctic, which no search party had ever succeeded in reaching. Nor did he ask about her strange, periodic absences. After the first time she disappeared, which caused him unutterable anguish, Lady Jane apologized profusely, saying she did not realize she had been gone long enough for Sir John to notice.

"Never fear, my darling," she had comforted him, touching his tear-stained face. "I shall not leave you. If I go, I shall always return, I promise you."

And she had kept her promise all these years — Sir John had long ago lost count of how many. What did it matter? He had his darling Jane's company and they were happy together. They wanted for nothing. Why should he worry about —?

"There!" Sir John leapt to his feet, spilling his tea in the process. "Did you hear it?"

Lady Jane looked up from her embroidery.

"Hear what, my dear?"

"Voices! I swear that's what it is!"

He grabbed his spyglass and ran to the edge of the deck. Lady Jane looked after him with concern.

"My dear, you know it's not good for you to get over-excited."

He looked out across the ice. Suddenly his knees began to buckle. He felt faint.

"Jane! Come quickly!"

She rushed to his side and grabbed his arm. He clutched the

side of the ship to steady himself and handed her the spyglass.

"Look! See for yourself! They have come! The rescue party. Our exile in this godforsaken land is over, my darling. We are saved!"

Lady Jane lifted the spyglass to her eye. Possibly Sir John was seeing a mirage, one of the visual tricks the Everlasting Ice was prone to play on clear, bright days like this. But no. There indeed seemed to be several tiny figures far out on the ice, moving unmistakably towards the ship.

"Can you make out anyone yet?" Sir John quizzed her. "Could it be Richardson, do you suppose? Or McClure?"

"I don't think so, my dear," Lady Jane said. "I must say they are moving in a most peculiar fashion. Not quite running, more like sliding along. And one of them appears to be ..."

"What?"

"A female."

"A female? That's impossible!"

"Another is ... I can't tell if it is male or female, but it appears quite short. Not much bigger than a child."

"Let me see that!" Sir John seized the spyglass. "What in blazes has gotten into the admiralty? Sending out a search party in such a state! Why, not one of them is even in uniform! It's a disgrace! And ... oh goodness! No. It can't be!"

"What is it, my dear?" Lady Jane grew alarmed at his tone.

He handed her back the spyglass. "Either I have gone completely mad, or they are being accompanied by a ... a bird!"

Lady Jane surveyed the party, now looming larger in the spyglass.

"You have not gone mad, Sir John. A bird it is. A loon, I believe."

✧

Molly arrived at the vessel well before the rest of them.

"It *is* a ship!" she cried. "The most wondrous ship I've ever seen! Now I can fulfil my destiny! This ship belongs to me, Pirate Molly!"

"Pirates! Great Caesar's ghost!"

At the sound of the deep male voice Molly whirled around. She thought it might be Jackpine, playing a trick on her. But the others were still some distance away.

"You! Knave! Don't move!"

Molly froze. The voice was coming from the deck of the ship!

"Turn around slowly with your hands above your head," ordered the voice. "Or I'll fire!"

Molly lifted her arms and slowly turned around to find the stout, grey barrel of a musket pointed right at her head. Staring at her from the ship's deck was a stocky, white-haired man who, despite his military dress and gruff tone of voice, appeared to be quaking with fear. At his side was a woman, only slightly younger, with large, warm brown eyes, dressed in an old-fashioned high-waisted gown. Molly watched as the woman calmly put her hand on the barrel of the musket.

"No need for alarm, my dear."

"You heard them! They are pirates!" the old man said insistently.

Molly feared that in his skittishness he might accidentally

fire. But the woman gently nudged the gun aside.

"You can see she is only a young girl."

"Molly!"

Peggy's voice came out of the distance, startling the old man, who swiftly turned and pointed the musket at the oncoming party.

"Stop or I'll shoot!"

"No, Sir John!" the woman cried out.

"We're not pirates!" Molly finally had the presence of mind to call out. "I swear! I was only pretending!"

The white-haired man slowly lowered the gun. Peggy, Gavi and Jackpine, still carrying Mi on his back, hesitantly approached the ship.

It was impossible to say which group was more dumbfounded at the sight of the other. Peggy and her companions could only wonder what on earth these two old people, dressed in quaint costumes, were doing on this ship sitting in the vast landscape of the Everlasting Ice.

For their part, the old couple were aghast at the motley crew before them: a young man and woman, a rather strange-looking, stiff-limbed young girl, accompanied by a lumbering avian creature with black and white feathers. Then, to their utter amazement, a tiny head poked out from inside a sort of sling on the young man's back. It was a child — a little girl so fragile and delicate she seemed to have no more substance than a wisp of hair.

Molly finally broke the silence.

"You see? We're not pirates. We mean you no harm."

Sir John managed to collect himself.

"Yes, of course. Please forgive me. How could I have been so wrong? Welcome, welcome. We are so glad to see you!" He briskly made his way down to the ice on the makeshift rope ladder that hung off the side of the deck. "You, sir ..." he said, striding over to Jackpine and saluting him, "I take to be the officer in charge. I see that you have had to discard your uniforms in the face of this land's hardships. Understandable, perfectly understandable. And you, sir ..." he turned to Gavi and saluted him, too, "you have no doubt donned this feathered suit as protection against the unforgiving cold. Ingenious solution, that! Difficult to maintain proper military decorum in such a get-up, but ingenious nonetheless! And you, madam ..." he gestured towards Peggy, "You must be exhausted from your long journey, and bringing along your children, no less! Highly unusual, sending women and children along on a search party! But the Royal Navy has its reasons, I suppose. Now," he said, rubbing his hands together, "you must come aboard and have some tea. My dear Jane, can we find some more cups for tea?"

"Yes, I'm sure we can," the woman replied. She turned to the group of them. "Please excuse me while I go below a moment."

"You'll have to forgive us, my friends," the old man went on. "It is so long since we have had visitors. But now sit down." He gestured to them eagerly as they made their way up the ladder. "Sit down and tell us all the news."

They were still too flabbergasted to speak, and they were still trying to make sense of the man's ramblings. Navy? Search party? Finally Peggy found the presence of mind to speak.

"News? What news?"

"Why, news of England, of course! We are starved for news of home!"

Molly piped up. "Oh, I see. You think we're from England. But actually we're from right here, in Notherland."

"Actually, from a bit south of here," Gavi added with his customary precision. "Below the Tree Line."

As the two of them spoke, a shadow seemed to cross the old man's face. For a few moments he was silent. Then he began to speak haltingly.

"I don't quite ... I'm afraid I ... You mean ...?"

Suddenly, without warning, he leaped towards Jackpine and grabbed him by the collar.

"You have come from England!" he screamed into Jackpine's face. "You are a rescue party sent by Her Majesty the Queen! Some calamity must have befallen you which has made you lose your wits. Now speak up! Who are you? What is your rank?"

The more the old man shook him, the more rattled Jackpine became. Finally the woman, who had just returned from below with more cups, stepped forward and lightly touched the old man's back.

"Please, my dear. Let the poor man go. You must not overexert yourself."

The old man slowly loosened his grip on Jackpine. The woman continued to speak in her calm, measured tones.

"You must consider the possibility that they are telling the truth, dearest." She turned to the others. "Please forgive us. Living in this land has been a terrible strain, and that, combined with Lord Franklin's bitter disappointment that you are not the rescuers for whom we have been waiting so long —"

"Did you say Franklin?" Peggy suddenly burst out. "Franklin, the Arctic explorer?"

"There, you see?" Sir John gestured triumphantly to his wife. "*She* knows who I am! They *are* from England! They must be the ones!" He turned to Peggy. "My apologies, madam. I realize now that you must be the one in charge. When I left England, you see, women were not even permitted into the military. Times have changed, I daresay!"

Peggy cleared her throat nervously. "Actually Lord, I mean, Sir, we're not from England."

"But if you're not from England, how do you know who I am?"

"Oh, well ... everyone knows about Lord Franklin."

"You mean my reputation extends beyond England?"

"Oh, definitely," said Peggy. "Your fame has spread throughout the world."

"Really?" said Sir John eagerly. "You don't say! Did you hear that, my dear? Why, that makes our long exile here almost worth it, doesn't it? I say, let's have that tea now. They may not be our rescue party, but we must still be hospitable!"

Lady Franklin began pouring the tea.

"Yes, Sir John, we must make the best of things, as we always have. Now, please," she said, turning to the others, "tell us about yourselves. What brings you to this lonely land?"

Molly and Gavi began to tell the Franklins about their journey to the Hole at the Pole, but Peggy's mind buzzed with questions. She knew she was the only one who fully realized the strangeness of what they'd encountered here. Sir John Franklin was a real-life, historical figure. His exploits — the voyages to the Arctic, his disappearance — had all taken place over a hundred and fifty years ago. How did he come to be here in Notherland? As for Lady Jane Franklin, Peggy clearly recalled that, according to *Our Wondrous North*, she had never come to the Arctic, indeed had never seen her husband alive again. So what was she doing here?

Gavi had said Notherland was changing, evolving more and more into an independent entity. Peggy couldn't wait to see what kind of explanation he would come up with for this latest wrinkle.

Molly was lifting Mi's face to show her to the Franklins.

"See? She's the last of the Nordlings — the only one not stolen by the Nobodaddy. We have to get to the Hole at the Pole and rescue the others before ... before it's too late!"

Sir John had listened to Molly's breathless tale with a certain scepticism.

"Well, I certainly have never heard of there being any sort of hole up at the Pole."

"There is!" Jackpine assured him. "I've been there!"

"As for this Noba ... this monster you speak of," Sir John went on, "that is news to me as well. Though it sounds a bit like that dreadful creature the Natives warned us about when we started up the Coppermine River years ago." He turned to his wife. "You remember my telling you that story, don't you, my dear? What was it called again?"

"A Wendigo."

"Yes, that was it, a Wendigo."

Jackpine suddenly snapped to attention. "That word sounds familiar to me. What's a Wendigo?"

"Well, according to the old legends, it is a monster with a heart of pure ice," began Sir John.

"Just like the Nobodaddy!" Jackpine exclaimed. "He has a heart of ice! What else do you know about this creature?"

Sir John hesitated. "It has a taste for ... well, it is something that really shouldn't be spoken of in polite company."

"A taste for what?"

Lady Franklin suddenly spoke up in a more definite tone of voice.

"Flesh. They have a ravenous craving for human flesh. But eating flesh, terrible though it is, is not the worst thing a Wendigo does. Some are tormented by an emptiness that can never be filled, but which they try to relieve, temporarily at least, by consuming the spirit, the living light of a human being. Stealing a soul, leaving a person a hollowed-out shell of his or her former self: that is the greatest evil. If your Nobodaddy is such a creature, he is a fearsome one indeed."

"But, my dear, those are just stories," scoffed Sir John. "You know perfectly well there is no such creature."

"There is," Jackpine said quietly. "I know."

Peggy could feel the simmering rage underneath his words.

Jackpine turned to Lady Jane. "You almost sound as though you've met the Nobodaddy yourself."

"Yes, my dear. I had no idea you were so familiar with Northern lore," said Sir John, looking curiously at his wife.

Lady Jane said nothing but stood up and briskly began to collect the dishes.

"You must all be exhausted," she said. "We insist that you accept our hospitality and spend the night here on the ship, before you continue on your journey."

"Yes," added Sir John. "You will need to be rested. Tomorrow you'll have to set your minds to figuring out a way to get across the Great Polar Sea."

They all gaped at him.

"You mean," Gavi cried, "there really is a Great Polar Sea?"

"See? You didn't believe me!" Jackpine said curtly.

"Mind you," Sir John said. "I have never laid eyes on it myself. Naturally, we have never ventured far from the ship, in case a rescue party should arrive. But all the great Arctic explorers, among whom I count myself, have proceeded on the assumption that beyond the Everlasting Ice lies a sea of open water, where the air is milder and the skies are free of icy blasts. By sailing across this Great Polar Sea, one might reach the Pole."

To Peggy, this was sheer wishful thinking, and she fully expected Gavi to dismiss it as such. But to her surprise, the loon's red eyes blazed with excitement.

"That means we can go to the Pole and not worry about freezing. Marvellous! Now all I have to do is figure out a way to navigate this Great Polar Sea. An enormous challenge, but I will rise to it!"

"Too bad we can't use your ship, Sir John," said Jackpine. "She's a beauty."

"Yes, that she is —" Sir John began, but he was interrupted by Molly.

"That's it!"

The others ignored her, but Mi piped up. "What, Molly?"

"Why not sail the *Terror* to the Hole at the Pole?"

Gavi shook his head. "Molly, do not be ridiculous."

"What's ridiculous about it?" Molly demanded.

"How would we get it there?" Gavi asked impatiently.

"We'll pull it!"

Gavi rolled his eyes. "Oh, Molly, there you go again —"

"We could!" Molly insisted. "This ice is so slick, all we'd have to do is give the ship a good push and get it to glide along, like a sled!"

Sir John spoke up with a note of enthusiasm in his voice.

"It's not totally farfetched, you know."

"What?"

"The young lady's idea. When we got trapped here in the ice, we tried to make our way out with enormous sledges piled up with rowboats, food, whatever would fit. We managed to pull them quite a ways. I'll wager one or two of those sledges were nearly as heavy as the *Terror*. Of course, there were more of us then. Many, many more of us. Then, one by one ..." His voice began to break.

Seeing his distress, Lady Jane rushed to his side.

"It's true there aren't many of us, my dear. But it's worth a try."

Sir John made an effort to collect himself.

"Before, there were only the two of us," Lady Jane went

on. "We could not contemplate such a thing. But with their help," she gestured towards the others, "it just might be possible to move the *Terror*. And if we succeed, you might finally achieve your life's dream ... of reaching the Pole."

As Lady Jane spoke, Sir John's spirits gradually rose, until at last his eyes lit up with excitement.

"Yes!" he cried. "Yes! We'll try it first thing in the morning."

Molly was exultant. "Hurray! I can't wait!"

Even Gavi was warming to the idea.

"Who knows?" he said to Sir John. "Maybe, if we can get the *Terror* to the Great Polar Sea, from there you can find your way back to ..." he had to pause a moment to think of the name, "England!"

Peggy couldn't contain herself any longer.

"What's the matter with all of you? The whole idea is crazy. Look at this ship. Look at us. We're not going to be able to move it an inch!"

"Ah, yes!" Sir John retorted, bristling with indignation. "That's just what all those nay-sayers tried to tell me when I left England: 'There is no such thing as your Northwest Passage, Franklin! You'll never reach the Pole in that ship! The whole undertaking is impossible.' Well, I didn't listen to it then, and I won't listen to it now."

Right, and look where it got you, Peggy almost said, but she kept quiet.

Molly stepped forward and gave the old man a snappy salute.

"We'll do it, sir. We'll give it our best shot!"

"That's the spirit," Sir John said firmly. "That's the kind

of attitude I like to see in a sailor. Now, what say we all turn in, so we'll look sharp first thing in the morning!"

Gavi turned to Sir John as he prepared to go below.

"What has become of Lady Franklin? Has she retired for the night?" he asked.

Sir John looked around and suddenly seemed flustered, for indeed Lady Jane was gone, though no one had noticed her leave.

"Yes, she ah ... I expect she has."

"Then please wish her goodnight for us."

"I will do so. Please, all of you, make yourselves comfortable."

And with that he disappeared down the narrow stairway.

❖

Sir John had offered them their choice of the officers' sleeping quarters below. But they wanted to keep an eye on Mi, and so they watched until she'd ascended safely into the pitch-dark sky. As they all sat huddled in blankets on the foredeck of the *Terror*, Peggy filled them in on what she knew of Lord Franklin's explorations. Molly was enthralled by the adventure of the story. But one thing mystified her.

"If he left England with two ships and a whole crew, what happened to all those men?"

Peggy looked at Gavi, who, of course, had already figured out the answer.

"The history books don't say," she said quietly to Molly. "They all must have starved or frozen to death. Or a combination. Nobody knows for sure."

"And where's the other ship? Why isn't it here, too?"

"There is much about this place, said Gavi, returning Peggy's look, "that is difficult to explain."

Jackpine had been sitting by himself, brooding. What Lady Franklin had said about the Nobodaddy had clearly stirred up memories of his time in the Hole, which he had thus far managed to keep at bay. Now, Peggy's account of the tragic outcome of the Franklin expedition seemed to make his mood even darker.

After a while he fell asleep, and Molly also snuggled up in her blanket, saying she'd had enough talking for one day.

Gavi and Peggy were left alone.

"What do you make of it all?" Peggy asked him.

"I must admit I am somewhat mystified," the loon replied. "All I can say with certainty is that the relationship between Notherland and your world — past, present, perhaps even future — is even more complex than I thought."

"What about Lady Franklin? Do you think she's some kind of spectre, conjured up by Sir John's mind to fill the loneliness?"

Gavi shook his head. "I think she is too much her own person to be a mere spectre. But I certainly agree that her presence here is mysterious."

"Did you notice how she seemed to vanish all of a sudden? And how she knew all about the Nobodaddy, even though Sir John had never heard of him?"

"I do not believe," Gavi said wearily, "that we will be able to solve all these mysteries tonight. I, for one, have done all the figuring-out I can do for one day."

The loon closed his eyes. As Peggy watched his head nod slightly forward, she brooded about the latest turn of events. What had started out as an adventure had become a much darker, more forbidding journey. The atmosphere on the ship seemed fraught with the suffering its former inhabitants had endured. No matter how feisty Sir John appeared, Peggy knew he had witnessed and lived through terrible things. Whether the Nobodaddy existed or not, real-life tragedy had invaded her world.

She felt a keen loneliness. She was the Creator, the one they believed had the power to save Notherland. But the longer she was in it, the more mysterious the workings of this world became, and the less able she felt to affect what happened to it.

She looked over at Jackpine, at his chest rising and falling softly with each breath as he slept. His arms were stretched out over the top of his blanket. As she drifted off, she had a fleeting moment of wondering how it would feel to be enfolded in a pair of human arms.

CHAPTER 6

The Good Ship Terror

WHEN PEGGY WOKE the next day, the sun was already high in the sky, and the others were up, bustling about the ship. Jackpine was attaching lengths of heavy rope to the ship's bow. Under Sir John's tutelage, Molly was tying the ends of the rope into a series of sturdy nautical knots, making huge loops into which the crew members — as they now fancied themselves — could insert their bodies. With luck, they would pull the ship forward until it built up enough momentum to skid across the ice. Even Mi was eager to help out, holding an end of rope that almost looked heavier than she was.

To Peggy it all seemed like so much wasted effort. The prospect of actually moving the enormous ship seemed even more ridiculous now, in the clear light of day. But she could see the others were oblivious to the folly of their plan. Somehow Molly's enthusiasm, combined with Sir John's wishful thinking, had swept them all along into believing it was possible — even Gavi, who should have known better.

Jackpine called over to Peggy.

"Morning! Sleep well?"

She just shrugged.

He looked at her quizzically. "Anything wrong?"

"Nothing, just ... This is crazy," she said grimly.

"What?"

"You know it can't work. That ship's never going to budge."

"Sir John said they did it before."

"There were a lot more of them! Look at us. What a crew! This whole thing's just a huge waste of time."

"You remind me of the people in the Hole," Jackpine told her. "You don't believe things can ever get better, so they don't. Well, give up if you want. I'd rather *do* something than sit around complaining."

As he stomped off, Molly let out a whoop of joy.

"Look! I did it!"

She pointed to a large knot that joined the two ends of the hauling ropes. Sir John came over and examined it with keen interest, joined by Gavi and Mi.

"Hmm, that's a pretty fair reef knot you've got there."

Molly beamed with pride.

"Next we'll move on to the bowline, one of the most important of all nautical knots."

"Yes, sir!" Molly gave him an eager salute. "I want to learn everything I need to know to make this vessel seaworthy! I can't believe it. For so long I've dreamed of being a pirate, and here I am, on a real ship!"

"You're becoming something far better than a lowly pirate," Sir John retorted. "Keep up the good work and you shall be a sailor in Her Majesty's Royal Navy!"

Peggy watched Molly stir with excitement at Sir John's

words. She wondered why she was the only one lacking enthusiasm. Whatever the outcome, the others at least had a mission, a shared sense of purpose. She wished she could just forget all her doubts and join the hubbub of activity. The crushing sense of loneliness she'd felt last night swept over her again. She longed to be relieved of the burden of responsibility, to just go back to her old life and forget all this.

"Jackpine is right."

Peggy was startled to hear a voice behind her. She turned to see Lady Jane.

"Were you talking to me?"

"It is far better to act than to complain."

Peggy was taken aback. Lady Jane's voice was sharp and brisk, much in contrast to the gentle, almost murmuring tones she used in speaking to her husband.

"I don't know what you mean," she replied.

"Why do you just sit here like a bump on a log?" Lady Jane moved closer and her tone became even more combative. "Go out there and help them!"

"Why should I bother?" Peggy retorted. "You know as well as I do it's hopeless."

"I admit the prospect looks awfully daunting. But this is a strange land. Unusual things happen."

"Even if by some miracle we can move the ship, how far is this Great Polar Sea?" Peggy pressed her. "How do we know it even exists?"

"The unknown is always a frightening prospect," Lady Jane replied. "But we must step into it if we want to move foward." Her tone softened a bit. "I know you are feeling downhearted at the moment ..."

She reached her hand out to Peggy, who abruptly turned away.

"How do you know what I'm feeling? Who are you, anyway?"

"Who do you think I am?"

"You're sure not Lady Jane Franklin."

"Oh?"

"You know what I'm talking about," Peggy continued. "You know perfectly well this ship's been stuck here for more than a century. What, is the old man some kind of ghost, hanging around the ship, refusing to admit he's dead? And how do you fit into the picture? Lady Franklin never came to the Arctic. She never laid eyes on her husband after he disappeared. So what gives? Who are you?"

Lady Jane opened her mouth, but before she could speak they were both distracted by shouts from the others.

"That's it!"

"We're ready to go!"

"Peggy! Come on over!" Jackpine called to her.

From the ship's great bow several loops fell, one for each of them except Mi, who was too small and light to be of help. Sir John's plan was that they would actually insert their bodies, one within each loop, which he believed would give them the most traction and power as they pulled forward on the ice.

Molly, Gavi, Sir John and Jackpine had each positioned themselves in one of the big loops. Only one remained unclaimed. Jackpine pointed to it and called to Peggy again.

"Come on! That one's yours!"

Peggy stayed where she was. Lady Jane spoke again.

"You must go and help. They cannot do it without you."

"All hands on the ropes," Sir John upbraided her mildly. "We need every body we have."

Peggy shook her head sullenly.

Now Lady Franklin's tone was as cold as the surrounding ice.

"Stop acting like a spoiled child! Get out there and do your part!"

"Fine!" Peggy snapped. "I'll show you just how ridiculous this is."

She vaulted down the rope ladder and out onto the ice, where she took up the last remaining loop and stepped inside it.

"When I give the signal," Sir John shouted at them, "pull with all your might! Ready, now? Heave, ho!"

For a few moments they all groaned and strained and pulled. But the ship didn't budge.

"Now let's not get discouraged," Sir John began.

Molly piped up. "Who's discouraged? Not me!"

"Let's try again. Everybody ready? Now! Heave, ho!"

"I thought I felt her give a bit that time," Jackpine said with forced optimism.

They all pulled with tremendous effort, once, twice, several times more. But nothing. The *Terror* was absolutely immovable.

Mi, sensing everyone's growing disillusionment, began to whimper quietly. Molly snapped at her.

"Stop carrying on! We have work to do!"

It was growing more and more obvious that the task was impossible. The ship was simply too huge, too heavy for the small group of them to move. Peggy turned and looked over her shoulder, ready to scream at Lady Franklin in frustration. But Sir John's wife was nowhere to be seen.

They made one or two more half-hearted tries. Finally Sir John let out a despairing sigh.

"I'm afraid that we —" he began, but was interrupted by an outburst from Peggy.

"Whooooa! What was that?"

They all turned and looked at her.

"What was what?" Gavi asked.

"I felt the strangest sensation under my feet just now."

"Like what?"

"I don't know, like ..." A surge of resolve shot through her, and she began to shout at them all. "Everybody pull! One more time! Pull!"

They looked at her, too mystified at first to move. Then they galvanized themselves and Sir John began his familiar refrain.

"Heave, ho! Heave, ho!"

Suddenly a tiny break appeared in the ice underneath Peggy. It felt to her as though a blast of warm air was shooting up through it.

"Look!"

The crack grew wider, and now the rest of them began to feel strange movements in the ice underneath their feet. Cracks were beginning to appear all over, accompanied by the same blasts of warm air.

"The ice!" Jackpine yelled. "It's breaking up!"

"Everyone on deck!" Sir John ordered.

They abandoned the ropes and began to scramble up the side of the *Terror*.

Peggy raced towards the ship, then suddenly remembered Mi. But Jackpine had already scooped the little sprite up and was carrying her onto the ship's deck.

Water started to gush up through the widening cracks, flooding the surface of the ice with great pools.

"We did it!" Molly shouted jubilantly. "We'll sail this channel all the way to the Great Polar Sea!"

CHAPTER 7

The Great Polar Sea

FROM THE DECK of the *Terror*, Mi looked out in all directions. The Great Polar Sea was so vast, its waters seemed to go on forever and ever. Mi was used to Lake Notherland. It had always seemed big to her, but at least you could see across it to the far shore. The Great Polar Sea was of another order altogether. Mi couldn't imagine that it had an end. And even if it did, she found it difficult to believe that they would ever reach it.

It had been more than a day since the remarkable phenomenon Gavi had christened the Warm Line. Mi recalled how she'd stood with the others on the deck, watching in amazement as the long gash opened up before them, releasing what felt like pulsing waves of warm air from underneath the ice. The entire crew had cheered with each loud *crack!* as the solid sheet of ice split in two and the ship slowly inched its way through the opening.

Gavi assumed that it was the power of Peggy's mind that brought the miracle about, that she had imagined a current of warm air under the ice. "That, combined with the ship's weight, could very well have made the ice give way underneath us," he said.

Peggy shook her head. "It just happened. I didn't have anything to do with it."

"But it is possible that your powers could be working without you being aware of it. What is that phrase? 'Your imagination is working overtime'? That could explain it," Gavi said, proudly parading his knowledge of the minutiae of everyday human speech.

"Perhaps it's a miracle, like the parting of the Red Sea," Sir John suggested.

None of them except Peggy knew what he was talking about. Sir John briefly told them the story, which he said was a miracle from a book called the Bible. Mi wondered how a sea could be red. As far as she knew, water was always blue. But she was too shy to ask Sir John about it.

Gavi would know. She reminded herself to ask him about it, and about her lucky bone, as well.

She took out a small cloth pouch and surveyed what was left of her "treasure." In the mad scramble onto the *Terror*, she had lost track of most of the stones. But a few of the prettiest ones remained, along with the smooth and slender tube that Peggy had said was a piece of animal bone. Gavi had told her once about how humans sometimes carried animal bones or teeth for good luck, and Mi decided that this would be her "lucky" bone. Why did it have holes? she wondered. Were they from the teeth of a bigger animal who'd tried to eat this one? She'd have to remember to ask Gavi how the holes got there.

Now they had finally left the vast plate of Everlasting Ice behind them and reached open water. So Jackpine had been right all along about the Great Polar Sea. Mi wondered how they could possibly tell which way the ship was going. Surely they would get lost! She was relieved to learn that experienced seamen like Sir John could steer a ship and chart a course using something called navigation.

In fact, Sir John was spending most of his time instructing Molly, on whom he had bestowed the rank of ensign, in the principles of navigation. He regretted having no uniform of the proper size for her, but he did bestow on her his very own, rather large, cutlass. Molly was thrilled, and promptly threw away the stick she'd been using as an imitation sword for so long.

Molly tried her best to follow Sir John's instructions, but she was finding the knots difficult for her stiff fingers. Then there were instruments like the compass and sextant, which were utterly baffling to her. And the ship's rigging looked like a chaotic mass of ropes and chains, no matter how carefully Sir John explained their organization and function. She tried to tell him that Gavi would be a much better navigator. But Sir John insisted that, much as he had become fond of Gavi and had come to respect his mental abilities, a loon was simply not fit to serve as an officer in the Royal Navy.

Sir John was also teaching Molly about the various signal flags that could be used to communicate with other ships. Molly found this a monumental waste of time, since everyone knew their chances of encountering another ship in the Great Polar Sea were virtually nil. But Sir John told her firmly that knowing about signal flags was an important part of being a well-rounded sailor. Worst of all for Molly were the drills, which he had her carry out several times a day. She had to march up and down the ship, deliver a proper salute, swab the deck and await Sir John's careful inspection. None of the others had to do any of these things, and Molly was beginning to resent it. Her initial excitement about learning to sail a real ship was slowly ebbing away as Sir John persisted in his attempts to mould her into a "model of military discipline," as he put it.

Mi watched Molly's growing disenchantment and frustration. The Nordling was so tiny and quiet, they often forgot she was there, but she noticed everything that was going on around her. The captain's efforts to bend Molly to his will reminded Mi of the way Molly herself had sometimes treated the Nordlings. Mi could understand Molly's resentment; it was how she felt when Molly tried to make her do something she didn't want to do. Though she saw some justice in Molly having to swallow a dose of her own medicine, the little Nordling still felt sympathy for the doll.

There was another relationship on board that intrigued and puzzled Mi. Did anyone else, she wondered, notice how Peggy and Jackpine always seemed to be watching one another? How they would stare at each another, then look away as soon as they'd notice the other watching? How they sometimes seemed to make excuses to be near one another? How they would speak to one another with a certain nervous excitement in their voices?

Mi sought out Gavi to ask him about it.

"Now that you mention it," he said, "their behaviour does remind me a little of mating rituals."

"What does that mean?" Mi asked him.

"It is something creatures do when there is a special bond between them, when they wish to spend time together and their feelings for one another are stronger than their feelings for others."

"Are Sir John and Lady Jane mates?"

Gavi smiled. "Yes, though they would not put it like that. Humans are not comfortable using the same terms for themselves as they do for animals — even though they are animals. The Franklins are husband and wife. Those are the human terms for mates."

"Yes," Mi said thoughtfully. "I can see that Sir John and Lady Jane have special feelings for each other."

"They are devoted to one another," Gavi agreed. "Lady Jane takes such good care of her husband. And when she is gone, he seems lost without her."

Mi was suddenly reminded of another question that had been weighing on her mind.

"Where does she go?"

"Who?" Gavi asked.

"Lady Franklin. Sometimes she just seems to disappear for awhile. Then she comes back again. Where does she go?"

"I do not know," Gavi replied. "I have wondered about that myself. But I suppose there is a simple explanation. Perhaps she goes below deck and carries out her wifely duties — cooking, mending, that sort of thing."

It occurred to Mi to ask Gavi why cooking and mending were considered a wife's duties and not a husband's, but her curiosity about such things was outweighed by the mystery of Lady Jane's absences.

"I wander about the whole ship," she told Gavi, "and I never see her below deck doing any of those things. I think she must go somewhere else."

Gavi shook his head. "That is impossible. How could she leave the ship? Where is there for her to go? Anyway, Sir John does not act as though there is anything unusual about her absences, and he is her husband. So we need not concern ourselves with it either," he said with finality.

It wasn't like Gavi to shrug off a mystery, to not probe more deeply until he found the solution to a puzzle. But Mi knew it was hard for him to admit when he didn't know the answer to something, so she changed the subject.

"Lord Franklin is trying very hard to make Molly into a good sailor."

"Yes," Gavi agreed. "But he does not seem to be having that much success. And frankly, I am amazed that she has gone along with it as far as she has. I have never been able to get Molly to do anything she did not want to do. She is the most stubborn creature I know."

"If she doesn't want to do those drills, why does he keep making her do them?"

"That is the problem," Gavi sighed. "Sir John has only one thing on his mind, making Molly into a good sailor, and he thinks she must try harder. He does not see that it is making her unhappy."

"If she's so unhappy, then why doesn't she just refuse to do it?"

Gavi smiled again. "Humans can be very hard to figure out sometimes."

"But Molly's not human."

"No," Gavi admitted. "But she would like to be. It adds up to the same thing."

They both stood silent for a few moments, staring out at the vast ocean.

"Gavi?" Mi said finally. "What will happen when we get to the Hole at the Pole? How will we set the Nordlings free?"

"Do not ask so many questions," Gavi replied brusquely.

Mi gazed at the water lapping at the side of the ship. It seemed to calm her mind, and she hoped it might be doing the same for Gavi.

She noticed something odd in the distance.

"Look!" she shouted.

Way off the starboard side of the *Terror*, something very large was rising slowly out of the water.

❖

Peggy's moods had been shifting wildly back and forth. She was constantly restless and found she had little appetite for the wonderful meals that magically appeared from the ship's galley. Sometimes she felt exuberant, elated. At other times the smallest thing would cause her to plummet into despair.

At first she didn't want to admit to herself that Jackpine was the focus of her moodiness. The longing to be near him. The constant thoughts of him when he wasn't around. The tingles of excitement she felt whenever she heard his voice or caught sight of his dark eyes and wiry, muscular body.

Okay, so she liked him. What good was that? He couldn't possibly feel the same way about her. Could he?

She watched him now, across the deck. He had that dark, faraway look in his eyes again. Was he brooding about the Hole? she wondered. Did she dare approach him in this mood? Would he open up to her?

He caught her gaze and nodded. Emboldened, she went over to him.

"Hi, what's up?"

He shook his head. "Nothing. Just thinking."

"We're really on our way, aren't we?" she offered, trying to make conversation.

"Yeah," he said pensively. "But I wonder if things are getting a little *too* easy."

Peggy let out a quizzical laugh. "What makes you say that?"

"You don't know the Nobodaddy," he replied. "You don't know what he's capable of. All I know is, we have to be ready for anything."

She opened her mouth to say something but was interrupted by shouts from the other end of the ship.

"Look!"

It was Mi's voice, followed by Gavi's.

"Peggy! Come quickly! There is something out in the water!"

Peggy raced towards the foredeck of the ship, followed by Molly, Sir John and Jackpine. They all looked in the direction Mi and Gavi were pointing. Sure enough, there was something very tall and slender sticking up out of the waves.

They all stood with their mouths open.

"What is *that?*"

"I cannot tell yet," Gavi said.

"It could be a fallen tree that somehow got washed out to sea," Jackpine speculated.

"Impossible," Gavi replied. "How could a tree stick up so high in this deep water, and what would it be doing so far beyond the Tree Line?"

"I'll wager it's an old mast," said Sir John briskly. "Perhaps from a ship that sank after an unsuccessful attempt to reach the Pole."

"It doesn't look smooth enough to be a mast, Sir John," Peggy pointed out. "It's hard to make out at this distance, but I can see some kind of ripples or bumps on the far side of it."

"Well," said Sir John, "we shall be able to tell better what it is when we get up closer. Ensign Molly!" he barked. "To the helm!"

"Not now. I want to watch from here," Molly objected.

"To the helm with you, on the double!"

"No!" said Molly defiantly.

Sir John's face was flushed with anger.

"This is rank insubordination!" he sputtered. "Do you have any idea of the penalty for —?"

But screams from the others interrupted Sir John's tirade. "Look!"

The thing bent over, then reared up even higher out of the water. Far from being an inanimate stump of wood, it appeared to be a living creature with a tremendously long neck, like some gigantic serpent. As it rose higher out of the water, great gushing whirlpools formed on either side of it. The protrusions Peggy had noticed looked to be scaly points, almost like sharp fins, which became progressively larger as they jutted out along the creature's neck and back. Before they had a chance to get a better look, it took a sudden dive and disappeared under the water, creating huge waves that crashed against the sides of the ship.

"What is it?"

"Some kind of sea monster!"

"Monster?" Mi whimpered, clutching Gavi's wing and burrowing nervously down into his feathers.

Jackpine turned to Sir John. "What kind of weapons have you got on this ship?"

Before Sir John could answer, Peggy broke in.

"Weapons? Why are we talking about weapons? We don't have any reason to think it wants to harm us."

"Whatever that thing is," Jackpine said grimly, "we'd better be ready if it shows up again."

"And if it attacks, we fight back!" said Molly excitedly, brandishing her cutlass. "I'm ready!"

"Oh Molly!" said Gavi, shaking his head. "What good would that sword be against a creature so large?"

Peggy interrupted them all.

"Shhh! Did you hear something?"

The others strained to listen. It sounded like a deep rumbling from the surrounding depths. They all stood frozen on the spot. It seemed to grow louder and louder. They could feel a vibration under their feet, and as the rumbling grew more intense the ship began to list sharply from side to side.

"Lord help us," Sir John prayed under his breath.

Suddenly a great wave spilled over the deck as the creature's head and long neck burst out of the water.

"Look out!"

The creature suddenly reared back, then snapped its head forward, its mouth sending out huge sparks the size of lightning bolts. Amid screams of fright, they all dove onto the deck to avoid the hot fiery sparks, which luckily seemed to dissipate in the air just above the ship.

"It's going to kill us!" Jackpine yelled as the ship continued to list perilously and the air around them crackled with flames.

"The musket!" Sir John shouted. He had been thrown back from the prow by the tossing and rocking of the ship, but now he grasped a cleat on deck and yelled to Peggy.

"There! Right beside you! The musket! Get it!"

Peggy looked around. There was a thick-barrelled rifle mounted just underneath the gunnel. She pried it loose, then held it out towards Sir John.

"No. You must do it! Raise it to your shoulder," he ordered her.

Peggy did so, awkwardly.

"Now aim!"

She pointed it upward towards the creature's head.

"Ready ..." Sir John called out, "... aim ..."

Before she could fire, Peggy lunged back onto the deck to avoid another volley of flames. The creature was now directly over her. She could practically see into its huge, snarling mouth. She scrambled onto her knees and lifted the gun back up to her shoulder. Aiming the barrel straight at the creature, she cocked the trigger.

"Hold it steady as you can while you release the trigger. Ready ... aim ... fire!"

She heard Sir John's voice, but her finger remained frozen on the trigger.

"Fire! *Now!*" Sir John bellowed. "What's the matter?"

Peggy took a deep breath.

Come on, pull the trigger.

But she couldn't bring herself to do it. She heard Molly calling to her.

"Go on, Peggy!" she shouted fiercely. "Blow its head off!"

She looked at the creature's head and imagined its flesh ripping apart at the shell's impact. The image sent a surge of adrenaline through her and she tightened her grip on the musket.

I can do this, she told herself. *I can do it!*

But something in her still held back.

Suddenly a loud blast sounded. Peggy watched as a shell went careening towards the monster's head. But her finger was still planted on the trigger of the musket. What happened? She hadn't fired!

She looked up, expecting to see the creature's flesh torn apart by the impact of the shell. But as soon as it was hit, the monster seemed to dissipate, like a puff of smoke into the air. After a moment there was nothing left of it, except for a strange band of light looming over the spot where it had been thrashing around seconds earlier.

Peggy heard a commotion on deck and turned to see Sir John and Molly rushing over to Jackpine, wide grins on their faces. What was going on? Then she noticed that another musket was cradled in Jackpine's elbow. He lifted it over his head jubilantly.

"Did you see that? One shot!" he shouted. "I nailed it my very first shot!"

So it was Jackpine who'd fired at the monster, not her.

She looked out over the sea. The strange ring of light now seemed to be moving along the surface of the water towards the ship. It hovered over the deck not far from where Peggy stood, and she watched in amazement as it lengthened to form a kind of column.

She tried to alert the others to the strange phenomenon, but they were busy congratulating Jackpine. When she turned back towards the shaft of light, she saw what appeared to be a solid form taking shape within it.

Then, abruptly, the light vanished altogether. There, on the exact same spot, stood Lady Jane Franklin.

CHAPTER 8

Gone

PEGGY WAS SHOCKED, not just by the eerie way in which Lady Jane had materialized on the deck, but also by the way she looked — weak, pale, almost ghostlike. She rushed over to her but was greeted with a dismissive wave.

"Go! Leave me alone! I am fine!"

Stung, Peggy started to back away, then looked straight at Lady Franklin.

"Sir John may pretend not to notice," she said, "but it's obvious to the rest of us that something pretty strange is going on here."

"I don't know what you mean," Lady Franklin answered.

"The way you come and go so suddenly. How do you do it? Where do you go?"

The older woman shrugged. "Where is there to go? About the ship, below deck ..."

"No! It's like you disappear into thin air. Where were you when we were fighting that sea monster? You had something to do with it, didn't you?"

"I?" Lady Franklin's laugh had a sarcastic edge. "Do I look like a sea monster to you?"

"I should have known better than to try and get a straight answer out of you," Peggy said testily. As she turned to go, Lady Franklin's voice brought her up short.

"You couldn't do it, could you!"

Peggy turned to face her. "Excuse me?"

"You didn't have it in you!"

"What are you talking about?" Peggy demanded.

"*You* should have fired the gun!" Lady Franklin said icily. "*You* should have destroyed the monster! Why didn't you do it?"

"What does it matter?" Peggy shot back. "The monster's gone, isn't it?"

"How can you prepare yourself for what lies ahead if you fail a simple test like this?"

"I haven't the faintest idea what you're talking about!"

"You will find out soon enough," Lady Jane said curtly.

Peggy was about to demand an explanation. But she saw a look of such overwhelming fatigue on Lady Franklin's face, that she thought the older woman might faint. Then she seemed to gather her forces, and marched over to her husband with a determinedly cheerful smile.

They were all still clustered around Jackpine. Though they found the monster's abrupt disappearance curious, it was clear to Peggy that she was the only one who had witnessed Lady Franklin's sudden, bizarre reappearance.

"I still can't believe that thing went down so easily!" Molly was saying, as she slapped Jackpine heartily on the back. "I was sure you'd have to shoot a bunch of those shells."

"Yes, the whole thing was a bit strange," Gavi allowed. "Do you have any idea what that thing was, Sir John?"

"There is a creature the Eskimos call Sedna," said Sir John. "A sea goddess. They call her the guardian of all the creatures of the sea, and say she is more powerful than our God. Which I dismissed as more mythical nonsense, of course. But I am no longer so certain of things as I was once. The important thing is," he said, patting his wife's arm reassuringly, "we are safe now."

Watching them all, Peggy felt a sudden surge of anger. *Hey, what about me?* she wanted to shout. *I would have shot it if I'd had the chance!* Of course, she was being ridiculous, she told herself. She'd had her chance. She had frozen up, and Jackpine had moved into the breach. After all, somebody had to do something.

Lady Franklin's words burned in Peggy's brain: *You failed the test. You should have fired the gun. Why didn't you?*

Why didn't I?

❖

"Gavi, do you know how these holes got into my lucky bone?"

Gavi was so obsessed with understanding the mysterious creature and how it fit into the cosmology of Notherland that he barely took note of Mi's question, and lumbered off muttering to himself: "A monster? A sea goddess? How could I have not known about it?"

Mi started to run after him, but Molly held her back.

"Better leave him alone for now. You know what he's like when he gets in one of his thinking moods."

Reluctantly, Mi admitted that Molly was right. Gavi was in no mood for questions.

"I'm going below deck to find Sir John," Molly told her. "I think you'd better come with me. Somebody should keep an eye on you all the time."

But Mi didn't want to go below deck. It was dark down there. There wasn't any place to play.

"I want to stay up here," she told Molly.

The doll hesitated on the stairway. "All right," she said finally. "I'll only be gone a few minutes. Be careful. Keep out of sight. And whatever you do — no singing! Not a peep! Understand?"

Mi nodded solemnly and watched Molly go below. She began skipping along the deck towards the stern. As she sprang past the main mast, she stopped suddenly. Up ahead were Peggy and Jackpine.

They seemed to be having an animated discussion, perhaps even an argument, Mi couldn't be sure. But she was struck by how the air around them seemed to crackle with currents of excitement. They seemed completely caught up in one another and oblivious to everything else.

Fine, she thought. *Everybody's busy with their own things.* She'd just play by herself. She was tired of them hovering around, constantly watching her. And she was sick of having to be so careful all the time. Right now, she was free to do just what she wanted.

Her eyes ran up the tall mast. It would be fun to climb up to the crow's-nest and look around. Maybe she could see all the way to the Hole at the Pole!

She began climbing up the shrouds, the way she'd seen Molly do under Sir John's tutelage. There was a bit of a wind up, but she'd be very careful not to get blown away. She'd hold on tight.

❖

Molly wondered why Sir John was taking so long below. She noticed that the door to his quarters was slightly ajar. Gingerly she approached it, and when she looked inside she could see Sir John from the back, slumped over his desk. The ship's log was open in front of him, and at first she thought he must be recording an entry. But then she saw a great shudder run through him, accompanied by a low moan, like weeping.

She wondered what to do. Did he wish to be left alone? Did she dare say anything, or even let on that she had seen him in this state?

She decided to tiptoe away quietly, but as she turned she brushed the door handle lightly, making the door knock gently against the jamb. Sir John raised his head and turned towards her. His eyes were swollen and red, and tears streamed down his cheeks.

Molly was overcome with embarrassment and immediately stiffened herself into a salute.

"Excuse me, Captain, sir. I didn't mean to disturb you."

She turned, intending to rush away, but Sir John called after her.

"Molly!"

She immediately noted that he hadn't prefaced it with "Ensign," as he usually did.

"Don't go," he pleaded, in a tone very different from the one Molly was used to hearing. "I cannot bear to be alone right now. Please ... stay."

"Sir?" Molly stood stiffly at attention at the end of the desk. "Would you like me to go fetch Lady Franklin?"

"I'm afraid that's not possible. Lady Franklin is ... gone!"

Molly watched transfixed as the great Franklin was overcome by racking sobs. He seemed to be in the grip of a terrible grief.

"Gone, sir? But I saw her only a short time ago ..."

He looked up, composed himself and pushed the log across the desk towards her. Molly looked at the latest entry, and, putting to use all of Gavi's painstaking instruction in reading, she managed to decipher the words.

Dearest,
I must be away for some time. But I shall do everything in my power to return to you. Our time together has been a great unexpected gift for both of us. Now the final phase of your great quest beckons. Do not lose heart! Know that I love you now and in eternity.

Yours, Jane.

"She is all I have, Molly. Now I am losing her. She is being wrenched away from me. Our life together is at an end."

"But Sir John, how could she leave the ship? Where would she go?"

Lord Franklin looked down and shook his head mournfully, as if he hadn't heard her.

"I knew it would come to this, one day. I knew it could not last forever. I am no fool. I knew she could not really be my Jane. She knew that I knew, but we never spoke of it. And I truly felt that a part of Jane's spirit somehow lived within her."

Finally he looked up and saw the look of bewilderment on Molly's face. He took a deep breath and began again in a calmer, more measured tone.

"You see," he went on, "I am perfectly well aware of the strangeness of my situation here. I know that my Jane passed on to her eternal rest many years ago, as did Crozier and Gore and the rest of my crew. I watched as they grew more hollowed-out and wasted with each passing day, their fingers and noses blackened by the freezing cold. I have seen such unimaginable horrors, Molly ..." He paused a moment, unable to continue.

"Dead. All of them. One after another. Because of my pig-headedness!"

"You? What do you mean, sir?" Molly asked.

"How many times I've castigated myself! If only I had not ordered the ships to turn south near Beechey Island, where we became trapped in the great ice stream that flows down from the Beaufort Sea! The Eskimos warned us against it, but stubbornly I clung to my planned route.

"I could not understand why I was being spared, why I had not passed on with all the others. I decided that was to be my punishment — doomed to stay alive, to live with the guilt of having caused so many to die. As the days and months passed, I grew more and more desperately lonely. To ease my loneliness I would speak with Jane, as if she were here with me. Gradually, I became aware of an uncanny feeling that I was no longer alone, that some other presence was nearby.

"Then one day, I woke up to find my beloved Jane sitting on the deck, calmly pouring morning tea. I thought she must be some kind of hallucination, that my thoughts of her had become so powerful that they had somehow conjured up her image. But as we spent time in each other's company, I could tell she was no mere figment of my imagination. She had a reality separate from mine. So I decided to accept her presence, without question, and to accept my fate, which is, apparently, for me to remain in this realm until I am called to meet my Maker. As long as I had someone so dear to pass the time with, it was all so much easier.

"I truly do not know whether I am living or dead, whether I am human or pure spirit. I only know that something is keeping me here, some force beyond my control or understanding. But now that I am faced with the prospect of losing my Jane for a second time ..."

Here Sir John's voice began to break, but he summoned his resources and went on.

"I no longer wish to remain here. I long to pass over into Eternity, so I can be with my Jane and find my final resting place. I cannot bear the thought of life without her!"

Molly listened, mesmerized, to every word of Sir John's tale. She feared that he would break down sobbing once again, but he simply sat with a look of unutterable sadness as a single tear made its way slowly down his cheek. Molly was overcome with pity. She had had no inkling of the trials Sir

John had been through, or of the deep well of feeling that lay beneath his stern military demeanour. What could she possibly say that would begin to offer him any comfort?

"But Sir John ..." Molly began, haltingly. "What about your great mission? The Pole ... we are so close!"

"I no longer care about reaching the Pole. Without the love of my life, nothing matters."

"If it would be of any help, sir," she added softly, "I will stay with you."

As soon as the words were out of her mouth, Molly felt like kicking herself. What an idiotic thing to say at a time like this! As if her companionship could in any way begin to make up for the loss of the most important person in Sir John's life!

Yet it made her realize that, however much they clashed with one another, she had become very attached to this man. Finally she had found someone in her life who took her seriously, who did not treat her like a mere plaything but demanded things from her, things that would help her live out her dreams! She wanted to plead with him not to pass over into Eternity, wherever that was, but to stay and keep serving as her Captain, her mentor, her teacher.

To her surprise, Sir John did not dismiss what she said. Indeed, he seemed to consider it quite seriously.

"It's true that you seem to have come here at an opportune time," he said. "Your presence here has given me a renewed sense of purpose, and one cannot live without a sense of purpose, anymore than one can live without love and companionship. The *Terror* has once again set sail, and she has a new crew. All this is good. Still ..."

He lingered on the last word, and Molly saw the pain flow back into his eyes.

"Sir John?"

"Yes, Molly?"

"Lady Jane did plead with you not to lose heart. And she promised to return — if she could."

Lord Franklin got to his feet, and for the first time since their conversation began, Molly saw a spark of the old, familiar Captain.

"You're right, of course. Here I am, moping about, when I should be making the best of things, as my Jane always counselled me to do. Thank you, Molly, for bringing me back to myself. You're a wise young girl."

❖

Mi looked out over the vastness of the Great Polar Sea from her perch on the mast. The wind whipped her around as if she were a piece of cloth, but she held on tight. To be up so high, to be part of something so unfathomably huge — Mi found it all exhilarating! Even being part of the RoryBory on a clear night was nothing like this. Now she was wide awake, and she was free! No RoryBory to fit into, no Gavi or Molly to tell her what to do. She felt like singing out her joy, but she reminded herself of Molly's warning.

She took out her lucky bone and waved it in the breeze. She was seized by an impulse to blow into it to see if it would make a noise. When she did, she was startled to hear how hauntingly familiar it sounded. This was not noise. It was music!

She blew into the bone again. Yes, it was unmistakably music. Not only that, it was her music, her note. It truly was her lucky bone! She couldn't wait to tell Gavi about this fascinating discovery.

A sudden chill coursed through her small body. She decided to scurry back down to the deck, before any of them realized where she'd gone and scolded her. As she began making her way down the shrouds, the wind grew stronger, and she had a sensation of some kind of force pulling on her, as if trying to wrench her away from the mast. Then she felt the dreadful chill again, and she thought she heard a sound like harsh laughter off in the distance.

She held on for dear life.

CHAPTER 9

The Bone Flute

JACKPINE WAS STILL EXHILARATED from shooting down the sea monster.

"Now I'm really going to take on the Nobodaddy. I can't wait to get back down in that Hole. I'm going to finish him off once and for all!"

"Listen to you," Peggy teased him. "The way you talk, you'd think you were going down there on your own."

"That's exactly what I plan to do."

"What are you talking about? I thought we were in this together."

"You don't think I'm going to let you go down there, do you?"

"Let?" Peggy sputtered. "Excuse me? Who are you to 'let' me do anything?"

"I've been down there. I know what to expect. You won't be able to handle it. He'll just eat you alive."

"Well, thanks for your concern," said Peggy sarcastically, "but I'll make up my own mind."

"Come on. You couldn't pull the trigger on that musket."

"I was about to!"

"Look, you don't know what you're dealing with here. It's like he gets right inside you and messes up your head. You can't tell his thoughts from your own. You've got to be tough with a creature like that. When the time is right, you have to go after him. You can't hesitate. Not for a second! I honestly don't think you've got what it takes."

"Why? Because I'm not all eaten up with hatred inside like you are?"

He looked into her eyes with a cold, hard stare.

"Maybe hatred is something you could use a bit more of."

They were interrupted by the sound of a prolonged tremolo wail.

Peggy felt a shiver run down her spine: the tremolo was the call Gavi used only in dire emergencies. They spied the loon at the base of the main mast and raced over to him.

"Gavi! What is it?"

But the loon continued to wail, utterly despondent. Finally Peggy reached over and touched his wing.

"Gavi, stop! You've got to use words and tell us what's wrong."

"She is *gonnne!*"

Before Peggy could say anything more, they heard Lord Franklin's voice behind them.

"Yes, we know!"

They turned to see the old captain and Molly emerging from the top of the stairs.

"Yes, she is gone, dear boy," Sir John continued. "But we must keep a stiff upper lip and make the best of it."

As though he hadn't heard a word Sir John said, Gavi

commenced wailing again.

"*Gonnnne!*"

"Who's gone?" Peggy demanded.

The old man looked as though he were fighting back tears as he handed her the ship's log with Lady Franklin's note.

"I'm afraid it's true. My dearest Jane has left us."

"Left?" Peggy and Jackpine both looked bewildered. "How?"

"She is *gonnnnne!*"

They were all becoming exasperated trying to make themselves heard over Gavi's persistent wailing. Then a terrible thought gripped Peggy.

"Gavi! Where's Mi?"

Now the loon lapsed back into his incoherent tremolo.

"Gavi! Speak words!" Peggy insisted. "Where's Mi?"

Gavi lifted one wing and seemed to be pointing to something near the bottom of the mast.

"I was with her just a few minutes ago!" Molly cried. "Maybe the Nobodaddy took her!"

"No way," Peggy said firmly. "She wouldn't have been stupid enough to sing, and that's the only way the Nobodaddy could have found her. She must be hiding somewhere."

Gavi gestured again towards the bottom of the mast, more insistently this time. Finally Peggy looked where he was pointing, and saw something lying there. She went and picked it up.

"It's one of those treasures she carries around — the one she calls her lucky bone."

Finally Gavi's speaking voice came back to him.

"Blow into it."

"Huh?" Peggy thought she couldn't have heard him right.

"Blow into the bone. You will see."

"See what?"

Peggy lifted the bone and placed it between her lips. Automatically, her fingers moved to cover the holes and suddenly, it was clear to her what Gavi was talking about.

She lowered the bone and looked at him.

"It's not, is it?"

"Yes," the loon replied quietly. "It is."

"What are you two talking about?" Molly cried impatiently.

Peggy raised the bone to her lips again, pressed her fingers over the holes and blew through it.

As air flowed through the bone, it released a distinctly musical tone.

Do ...

She moved her fingers, leaving one of the holes uncovered this time, and blew again.

Re ...

Then she blew a third time, leaving both holes uncovered.

Mi ...

"So that's how the Nobodaddy discovered her!"

"The bone is a kind of flute. I was trying so hard to figure everything out," Gavi cried bitterly, "but I was not paying attention to the most important thing of all! Mi tried to show me, but I kept ignoring her. And now she has been snatched away. The last of the Nordlings is gone! We are all doomed. Notherland is *dooooommed.*"

"It's my fault!" Molly burst out. "I shouldn't have left her alone on the deck!"

And Gavi wailed as if his heart would break: "*Gonnnnne! Dooooommed!*"

❖

For the next few hours they all worked furiously, trying to sail the rest of the distance across the Great Polar Sea as quickly as possible. Molly took the helm, and Peggy and Jackpine trimmed the sails, while Sir John scoured the hold of the ship for fuel, hoping to get the *Terror*'s old coal-fired engine going again. But it was no use. The entire store had been used up long ago.

Gavi racked his brain, going over every conceivable possibility, trying to come up with a plan. Maybe if he thought hard enough, if they could sail the *Terror* fast enough, they'd somehow find a way to reach the Pole before nightfall. As long as there was daylight, there was still hope.

But as darkness descended, though the Great Skyway sloped out of the sky as it always did, there was not a single Nordling to make the journey upward.

On the deck of the *Terror*, the gloom was almost palpable. Gavi began to berate himself.

"How stupid I am! I thought I knew so much, but I know nothing!"

To complicate matters, Sir John was still overcome with grief at the loss of his wife. Molly ran back and forth between Sir John and Gavi, trying to comfort and reassure them both. But Peggy could see that underneath the doll's frantic efforts to raise their spirits, she was waging a fierce battle to keep from crying herself.

The spectre of almost certain failure only made Jackpine more furiously determined to make the ship go faster. But as he worked, he had a hollow look in his eyes, one that reminded Peggy of the odd feeling of familiarity she'd had when she first met him.

Peggy felt the gloom seeping through the pores of her own skin. She looked around. The *Terror* was now drifting aimlessly in the open sea. They had given up. It was all over. Notherland was doomed to extinction.

She was the Creator, but never had she felt so utterly powerless. The darkness deepened around her. It was as if the Hole had already swallowed them up.

She took out Mi's bone. It felt strange to hold a flute in her hands again, even one as simple as this. Her fingers spontaneously cradled around the holes in the bone, as if they felt completely at home there. She lifted it to her lips and blew a sustained, unadorned note, sending out her sorrow in a deep, mournful cry over the vast ocean.

Then she tucked the little flute into her pocket and fell into an exhausted sleep.

❖

It wasn't lost after all!

She was standing in front of a store, holding her flute case. There was a sign in the window: Used Musical Instruments Bought and Sold.

She went inside. It wasn't a brightly lit store like Around Again, but a small, dingy pawnshop. She walked over to the counter and laid her flute case on it. But when she opened the case, the man behind the counter laughed out loud.

"Honey, this is just an old bone!"

She looked and saw with a shock that it wasn't her silver flute, but a plain bone flute with jagged ends.

She looked around. The pawnshop was filled with other customers, and they were all laughing heartily and pointing to the bone flute. Humiliated, she rushed to the door, leaving the case sitting on the counter.

Someone was coming in the door of the pawnshop. It was Lady Jane! No one in the shop seemed surprised by the strange way she was dressed. In fact, no one seemed to notice her at all.

"You must go back and get your flute," Lady Jane said.

"Why? It's just a worthless hunk of junk!" Peggy said bitterly.

To her surprise, Lady Jane put her arms around her and began to murmur comfortingly.

"You must not be discouraged, child. It's a long day. A very, very long day."

❖

When she jerked awake, Peggy felt a momentary sense of comfort from the dream. Maybe it was a sign that things really would turn out all right. But then she could hear the man's mocking laughter in her ears. And what did Lady Jane mean by that odd phrase "It's a long day," instead of "It's *been* a long day"?

She realized that she'd only drifted off for a short time, since night hadn't yet come. As she watched the sun drop lower and lower on the horizon, she felt sure that the dream was nothing but wishful thinking, an attempt to give herself one last thread of hope. One thing was certain: that thin crescent of sun was about to disappear. Strangely, her terror of night had receded. Now she was only aware of a feeling of detached curiosity.

What would happen at the moment the sun was swallowed up completely? Would Notherland itself instantly disappear? Would it grow smaller and smaller, or slowly fade away, like a scene in a movie? What would happen to Peggy herself? Would she be annihilated, or abruptly thrown back into her other life in the "real" world? How strange — just as Nother-land sat poised on the edge of total extinction, it seemed far more real to her than that other life.

The tiny crescent hung there, as if in suspension. Any moment now ...

Peggy blinked her eyes, and it seemed in that fraction of a second that the crescent had grown slightly larger. Were her eyes playing tricks on her?

As she watched, the sliver-sized sun did seem to be growing larger, even moving back above the horizon. But how? It couldn't be ...

"*It's a long day.*"

A long day.

"*A very, very long day ...*"

"Gavi!"

The loon lumbered across the deck towards her.

"What is it?"

"Gavi!" Peggy was so excited she could hardly speak. "Do you realize what day this is?"

Gavi stared at her, uncomprehending.

"Look!" she said, pointing to the horizon. "The sun didn't set! I swear it didn't! It's rising again!"

Roused by the commotion, the others came running, too.

"The Solstice!" Gavi cried. "The endless day! The one day of the year when the sun does not set in Notherland! What a dummy I am for not thinking of it!"

He let loose with a wild, ringing loon-laugh. Sir John, Molly and Peggy looked at one another, then suddenly began to jump up and down, screaming and hugging.

"We're saved!" Molly cried.

"*Saaaaaved!*" Gavi chimed in.

"Not quite," Sir John pointed out. "But at least now we've got a fighting chance."

"Not much of one," Peggy added. "The days start getting shorter now. Without the RoryBory, as soon as that sun drops below the horizon, even for half a second, Notherland is history. That means we've got less than twenty-four hours to get to the Pole and figure out a way to free the Nordlings." She called over to Sir John. "What's our position?"

"Thunderation if I can tell!" the old captain said with exasperation. "The farther north we go, the worse havoc that blasted Pole plays with my instruments!"

"Can you figure out how soon we'll arrive at the Pole?"

Sir John shook his head. "Not precisely. But it can't be far."

"True north, full speed ahead!" Molly called out heartily.

"That's what I like to hear!" replied Sir John.

Peggy looked around. "Wait a minute! Where's Jackpine?"

They looked at one another. In all the excitement, they hadn't even noticed his absence.

"Jackpine?" Peggy called out. "Jackpine?"

"Look!" Molly gasped as she pointed up ahead.

The *Terror*'s lifeboat, which had been lashed to the side of the foredeck, was missing. On the same spot there was a single sheet of paper, tacked down with a nail.

Molly retrieved the paper and handed it it to Peggy. She read it quickly, then silently handed it to Sir John, who read it out loud.

Dear Peggy and crew of the Terror —
I've gone on by myself. I can get there faster in the small boat. This way there's a chance I can still get to the Pole in time to get the Souls out of there, and the Nordlings, too. At least this time I don't have to swim! Turn back while you still can. Don't worry about me. Whatever happens, it was worth it to be free for a while, and to know you. Farewell.

Your good friend, Jackpine.

As he read, Peggy fought to control the confused jumble of emotions washing over her. Giddy excitement, that he'd addressed her by name and not the others. Anger, that he was shutting her out, trying to do it all himself. Anguish, that he'd left so abruptly, without saying goodbye, even though she might never see him again.

When Sir John finished, Molly was the first to speak. "He wants us to turn back!"

Gavi shook his head sadly. "Jackpine is very brave, but very foolish. He was defeated by the Nobodaddy once before. Alone, he may not survive a second attempt."

"Yeah, he needs our help!" Molly declared. "I want to keep going! Don't you, Peggy?"

Before Peggy could answer, Sir John's booming voice broke through.

"Ahoy! Ahoy!"

They all looked in the direction he was pointing. Off in the distance was a huge, white, irregularly shaped object.

"What is it?" Molly cried excitedly. "Land? Are we at the Pole?"

The object was tearing towards the ship at great speed. As it grew closer, Peggy could make out sharp, jagged points of ice jutting out at its base, like the blades of an enormous jigsaw.

"Iceberg!" she yelled. "Dead ahead!"

Now it was headed straight for the *Terror*.

❖

It was only Molly's quick thinking and skilful work at the helm that prevented the iceberg from taking a deep gash out of the ship. She swerved the *Terror* sharply to port just as the iceberg was bearing down on it, causing the ship to list badly.

It happened so quickly that the others barely had time to react. They all watched, with gaping mouths, as the huge hunk of ice barrelled towards them, and they grabbed on to whatever they could as the ship leaned perilously to one side. As soon as Sir John saw that the iceberg had bypassed the ship and they were out of danger, he called out to Molly.

"Hell of a steering job, Ensign Molly!"

But it quickly became clear that their relief was premature.

"Look!" Peggy pointed off in the distance.

There were more icebergs, perhaps dozens more.

"They must be breaking off from the ice around the Pole!" Gavi said.

"Good heavens! How are we going to steer around all of them?" Sir John cried.

He had barely finished his sentence when his voice was drowned out by a cacophony of smashing, scraping and grinding noises up ahead of them.

"They're crashing into each other!" Peggy shouted, barely making herself heard. "Here they come! Look out!"

Two icebergs were coming at the *Terror*, one on either side. It seemed certain that the ship would be crushed between them. Sir John grabbed the helm as Molly dove for the mainsheet, pulling at it and catching a strong gust of wind that propelled the ship forward with such force it almost lifted it out of the water. They all looked behind and saw the two icebergs collide, creating an explosion that sent shards of ice spewing into the air around them.

As more of the huge ice-forms swarmed around the ship, sometimes looming right above their heads, Molly took the helm and steered like an experienced sailor. Her reflexes seemed almost supernaturally sharp. With Sir John at her side, guiding her every manoeuvre, even her blind eye caused her no problem.

Just when Molly's concentration was beginning to give out, the sea around them grew calmer and quieter, and the icebergs began to recede behind them.

The great rim of the Hole, with billowing puffs of smoky vapour rising out of it, appeared before them.

"It looks as though Hell has frozen over," Gavi said.

"Is that what I think it is?" Molly cried, pointing ahead.

Peggy's heart leapt when she saw the *Terror*'s lifeboat, along with a pair of oars, lying beside the rim of the Hole.

CHAPTER 10

The Hole at the Pole

SIR JOHN STOOD ON THE DECK of the *Terror*, looking at the great gaping Hole as it spewed what looked like smoke into the air.

"There it is," he said quietly, "the destination that I have spent a lifetime striving to reach. I thought I would feel triumphant when this moment finally arrived. But without my Jane at my side, I ..."

The other three looked at one another in silent sympathy. Peggy, weighed down by the crushing disappointment of finding the rowboat but no sign of Jackpine, understood how the captain was feeling. Finally, she spoke up.

"Someone has to be first to set foot at the Pole. Would you like to do the honours, Sir John?"

Gavi surveyed the expanse of smooth coal-black terrain that surrounded the rim, where the ship had run aground.

"I cannot tell what the surface is made of," he said dubiously. "Perhaps someone smaller than Sir John should test it out first."

"Me!" Molly piped up. "I'm the lightest."

"That's exactly why you *shouldn't* go first," Peggy said

firmly. "Just because it holds you doesn't mean it will hold us."

"A brilliant piece of reasoning," Gavi said. "I should have thought of it myself."

Before anyone could say another word, Peggy hoisted herself over the side of the deck and down the rope. The others all sucked in their breath, fearful that it would break, that she would go crashing into the frigid waters of the Polar Sea or whatever else lay beneath the forbidding shelf.

There was an audible sigh of relief as she landed with a thud.

"It's solid, all right." She slammed one foot hard on the surface. "Solid as a rock. It's ice."

"Of course!" Gavi blurted out. "Ice so black that none of us recognized it as such. Black ice is the hardest, most unforgiving kind. It makes sense that we would find it here at the Pole. But right next to open water? How can that be?"

"Another of the Pole's mysterious reversals, no doubt," offered Sir John. "Hopeless to try to explain such things."

"But it does suggest an explanation for this mysterious vapour," Gavi went on, as one by one they hoisted themselves onto the black ice. "That smoke we are seeing is not from fire but from ice. The Hole must consist, at least in part, of what is called 'dry ice' in your world," he said, nodding in Peggy's direction. "So there is no inferno in there. Just more cold. Dark, unutterable cold."

Peggy strode purposefully across the ice towards the rim of the Hole, followed by the other three. As they approached it, great swells of vapour grew thicker and thicker around them, like a fog. At times they could barely see one another. But they groped their way to the very edge of the Hole and peered down into it.

Sir John spoke first.

"It looks like a bottomless pit."

"Every hole has a bottom," Gavi pointed out. "A bottomless pit is a physical impossibility, even in Notherland. Now, of course, there might be other universes where such a thing ..."

"It's just an expression, Gavi," Peggy stopped him.

"Yes, of course. I knew that," Gavi said sheepishly.

"But where is everybody?" Molly interrupted. "Where are all the Souls Jackpine talked about?"

And where is Jackpine? Peggy added silently to herself. *Is he down there? How will we find him?*

"I'll bet he's got them all stirred up!" Molly answered her own question. "I'll bet right now they're all way down there, crushing the Nobodaddy!"

"Well, there's only one way to find out," Peggy said, as she began to lift one leg over the rim."Who's going with me?"

"Me!" Molly declared firmly.

"And me," Gavi added, with somewhat less conviction.

"This is my great adventure!" Molly cried. "I can't wait!"

Peggy looked at the old captain. "What about you, Sir John?"

He shook his head.

"It appears I am the only member of this crew who is of truly sound mind, because I have no desire whatsoever to descend into that forbidding pit. My life's goal has been to reach the Pole, and now I have achieved it."

Peggy grinned at him. "That's good, because someone ought to stay with the ship. If we do manage to get out of here with the Nordlings and Jackpine and all those other trapped Souls, you'd better have the *Terror* ready to sail out of here like a bat out of hell."

"A most colourful, if slightly blasphemous, simile," Sir John observed. "I assure you I will be thoroughly at the ready. When the time comes, the *Terror* will show that she can fly more swiftly than any bat."

Molly looked up at Sir John with concern. "Are you sure you don't mind being left alone?"

"My child," he said, addressing her with that term of endearment for the first time, "being alone is a thing with which I am very familiar. Do not worry about me. When you return, I will be here to welcome you."

Peggy looked at Molly and Gavi. "Well?"

Molly peered into the Hole.

"It's pretty dark. But I'm not afraid!" she added quickly.

In the dim light Peggy was able to make out a narrow ledge along one craggy wall, which seemed to be a pathway down into the Hole. She took a deep breath.

"Let's go."

As the three of them prepared to scramble over the rim of the Hole and onto the upper reach of the ledge, they bade Sir John farewell. Gavi and Peggy shook the old man's hand, and Molly flung herself onto Sir John's chest. He wrapped his arms around her, and they embraced one another tightly for a moment. Watching them, Peggy suddenly recalled reading in *Our Wondrous North* that when he'd embarked on his last, fateful Arctic expedition, Lord Franklin had left behind not only his wife, but a daughter as well.

✧

Their descent, initially at least, was uneventful. The air was bitingly cold, but not unbearable. Once their eyes adjusted to the darkness of the Hole, they found they could see well enough to make their way — especially Gavi, whose red eyes were adapted for seeing through dark waters at night. Not that there was much to look at. As far as they could make out, the Hole was little more than a dark, craggy, funnel-shaped cavity that extended deep into the earth.

The three of them walked mostly in silence. After a while Peggy began to wonder if things were going a little too smoothly. Where was the Nobodaddy? Did he know they were there? Why was he letting them go on unimpeded?

Gavi's voice broke in on her thoughts. "What was that?"

"What?"

"I thought I heard something," Gavi replied.

"There!" Molly volunteered. "I hear it, too. It sounds like voices farther down. Do you think they're Souls?"

"It seems likely." Gavi turned to Peggy. "What do you think we should do?"

She shrugged. "Let's go see. It's about time we came across some signs of life down here."

As they made their way farther down the ledge, the voices grew louder, shouting angrily, in barely coherent outbursts.

"— all your fault!"

"If you hadn't been so stupid —!"

"I hate you!"

After a few moments, Peggy began to call out.

"Hello? Hello!"

She could barely hear herself over the noise. She tried again.

"Hello? Hello down there!"

A volley of shrieks echoed off the walls of the Hole.

"What's *that?*"

"Did you hear something?"

"No, you idiot."

"I heard it!"

"Oh, great. Another one!"

Peggy shouted, "Could you all shut up a second and listen?"

"We've come to help you!" Molly added.

"There's more than one of them!" one of the voices shouted to the others.

Peggy began to yell over the voices, trying to explain who they were and why they had come to the Hole. But it was difficult. After every few words, a volley of shouts would go up — arguing, accusing, insulting.

"Just hear me out!" Peggy tried again. "I'm trying to tell you that we've come to rescue you. All of you."

At that, a roar of bitter laughter rose up from the darkness of the cavern.

"Rescue? Ha! That's a good one!"

"That's what the last one said and look what happened!"

"What last one?" Peggy feared they might be referring to Jackpine. "Who are you talking about?"

"The one who came through earlier."

"He was the stupidest of all!" said one bitingly. "He escaped the Hole once, and he *came back!*"

"Where is he?" Peggy demanded. "What happened to him?"

"Who knows?" shouted one.

"Who cares?" yelled another.

Listening to their harangues, Molly grew more and more angry. She began shouting at them at the top of her lungs.

"You're all idiots! We come here to help, and all you can do is blame us, or one another. You're either completely crazy or completely stupid!"

Gavi was becoming more and more disheartened by what he was hearing. He winced at the volley of shouts, as if they were slaps in the face. Such meaningless, self-destructive behaviour shocked and distressed him. He turned to Peggy.

"What is the matter with them? Why are they acting this way? Do they not want to be rescued?"

Peggy shook her head.

"Maybe not. It must be like Jackpine said — they've gotten so used to being miserable they can't imagine anything else."

"But that makes no sense!" Gavi cried. "Heaping scorn on people when they try to help you makes no sense at all. And listen to them — they are cruel to one another when they should be kind, and help one another, and make the best of their situation. They only make it worse. I do not understand this behaviour at all!"

Peggy was troubled by Gavi's extreme distress. She'd never seen him in a state like this. She decided they'd better move on before these raging Souls threw him into an even darker mood.

"Let's go."

"But we must try to talk some sense into them!" Gavi said with an air of desperation, as if his own mental well-being depended on getting them to listen to reason.

"Gavi, there's nothing we can do for them. You can see for yourself. They just won't listen."

"Yeah!" Molly agreed. "They're not interested. So long, idiots!"

The three of them continued down the path, the angry shouts growing fainter and fainter in their ears. When they were finally out of earshot, Peggy breathed a sigh of relief. Hopefully, now, Gavi would calm down and regain his sense of perspective.

Peggy turned to look at him. There was an odd look in the loon's eyes, and his beak appeared to be stuck in a half-open position. He seemed to be trying to speak, but nothing was coming out.

"Gavi? What's wrong?"

He looked at her with a panicked expression. She could see that he was indeed having difficulty speaking, and the prospect was terrifying him.

He continued to strain, trying to form some words and get them out. Then suddenly a great rush of sounds came out of his beak. At first, it sounded like nothing but gibberish.

Little by little, Peggy was able recognize words in the babble.

"... no, no ... terrible ... makes no sense ... cannot ..."

"You can't what, Gavi?"

"Cannot ... go ... on!"

Peggy was stunned.

"What are you saying?"

"No sense ... If I go on ... lose my mind!"

He looked to be in the grip of a nameless terror, and it was clear to Peggy that he was in no condition to continue their journey.

"It's all right, Gavi. You don't have to go any farther."

Molly looked at her, aghast, but before the doll had a chance to object, Gavi collapsed into loud wailing.

"*Soooorrryyy!* Let you *dooooowwnn!*"

Molly tugged at Peggy, trying to make herself heard over Gavi's cries.

"We can't just leave him here, Peggy! What'll we do?"

For an instant, Peggy felt like she was going to explode. She was the one they turned to every time! She was the one who supposedly had all the answers. She didn't know how long she could stand it!

But she knew she couldn't afford to give in to her frustration. She had to somehow get Gavi calmed down. They had to keep going. What should she do?

A thought came to her. She went over and softly touched his feathers.

"Gavi? You know Molly and I have to go on. Do you

think you can make it back to where the Mad Souls are?"

"Are you crazy?" Molly exclaimed. "He can't go back there!"

"He'll be worse off staying here, all alone," Peggy replied. "He'd lose his mind for sure. Gavi?" She moved closer to him. "I think you should go back and try to talk to the Mads. I think they might listen to you."

Gavi looked at her long and hard.

"But you said yourself that they are not interested in anything we have to say."

Peggy didn't believe for a minute that the Mads would change their behaviour. But she figured it would be better for Gavi to have a task, something to focus his mental energies on.

"I was wrong. I think they would be interested, if somebody got to know them and took the time to explain things to them. You're just the person to do it, Gavi. If anybody can talk sense into those Mads, it's you."

The loon's red eyes began to grow a bit brighter.

"Yes, I think I see what you are getting at. It makes sense."

Peggy and Molly both nodded vigorously.

✦

Gavi insisted that he could find his way on his own, that his red eyes could see well enough in the dark. But the other two wouldn't hear of it, and they backtracked with him up the path. When they got within earshot of the Mads, Gavi indicated that he wanted to go the rest of the way by himself.

"I believe that I can startle them into attention with my

tremolo call. And I think they will be more open to my presence if they sense I am alone."

Peggy immediately agreed. She recalled how Molly had only egged them on with her taunts, and she saw that Gavi didn't want to risk setting them off again.

For a moment, Molly stood stubbornly, unwilling to part from Gavi.

"Go on," he said to her. "Go with Peggy. You wanted to live out your adventure to the very end, remember? We will see one another soon."

It was wrenching for Molly to say goodbye to the loon, and watching his black-and-white body lumber up the path and disappear into the darkness was almost unbearably painful. She and Peggy resumed their descent in silence.

"Do you think he's all right?" Molly asked anxiously after a short time.

"He's okay, Molly. You know Gavi. Once he gets going, they won't be able to shut him up. He can debate his way out of anything."

Though Peggy felt keenly the loss of Gavi's company, she realized that, with his sensitive nature, he was better off staying behind. Whatever awaited them down below would probably upset him even more than the Mads had. But Molly was different. Her faith never flagged. Peggy knew she could count on the doll.

Molly spoke up again. "Did you hear something?"

"No," Peggy replied. "What was it?"

"I'm not sure ..."

They both listened as a faint crescendo, like some

drawn-out wail, rose up from the great cavern.

"Strange," said Peggy. "If I didn't know better I'd say it sounded like Gavi."

"But Gavi's back with the Mads."

They moved farther down the path, then stopped in their tracks as a new volley of wails and anguished cries began to rise up, reverberating from deeper in the Hole.

"That's for sure not Gavi," Molly said with some relief.

As they descended farther it became clear that they were approaching another colony of Souls. Peggy felt her hopes rise again, wondering, *Is Jackpine with them?*

These voices contained no hint of anger or accusation. Instead, they filled the atmosphere of the Hole with unrelenting echoes of anguish, pain and sorrow.

"They're sure not Mads," the doll's voice broke in. "Sads is more like it."

They moved closer to the voices, and as she had with the Mads, Peggy called out to explain who they were and why they had come. As soon as the words were out of her mouth, a mournful cry rose up.

"Not another one!"

This time, Peggy knew who they were talking about.

"Who? What happened to him?"

More cries.

"He left to find the Nobodaddy."

"But it was no use!"

"He got our hopes up for nothing."

"Now things are worse than ever!"

"We're doomed to languish here."

"No love, no hope, no love, no hope."

Peggy had never heard such utter despair. She looked at Molly, who was now trying to call out over the Sad Souls' din.

"Don't give up hope! If you just give up you won't be able to get yourselves out of here when the time comes!"

"Go back where you came from!"

"While you still can."

"You can do nothing for us."

"No one can."

Their cries managed to completely drown her out.

Peggy put her hand on Molly's stiff shouder. She could feel the doll fighting back angry tears.

"What's the matter with them?" Molly cried out. "Can't they see that giving up is the worst thing they can do? I never give up hope. I *never* stop trying."

Peggy saw that the Sads' despair was having a powerful effect on Molly. The Mads had brought out her natural feistiness: they had dished out abuse, and she'd dished it back. But the unrelenting anguish of the Sads was something Molly had never witnessed before. Such extreme suffering frightened her. She shut her eyes tightly and covered her ears, trying to block out their cries. She looked so upset that Peggy figured they had better get out of earshot of the Sads quickly, before Molly broke down completely.

With difficulty, she pulled the doll along the path. Molly steadfastly held her hands over her ears. When they had gone far enough that Peggy could barely hear the Sads, they stopped, and she gently uncovered Molly's ears.

"There. Isn't that better?"

She was shocked when the doll shook her head. Molly's eyes brimmed with tears.

"I can still hear them!"

"You couldn't, Molly. They're way behind us —"

"You don't understand. That's not it."

"What?"

"I can't get the sound out of my head. It's like they're crying inside me!"

"Maybe it's an echo," Peggy offered anxiously. "Give it time to die down."

The doll shook her head more vigorously.

"It's not an echo. I told you, it's inside me."

"Then the best thing is to put more distance between them and us," Peggy said, and she started walking again. But Molly pulled on her arm.

Peggy looked quizzically at her.

"What is it?"

"I can't," Molly said.

"You can't what?"

"I can't go any farther," responded the doll, tearfully.

"But Molly, we have to keep going."

"You go on without me," she said solemnly. "I'll go back to the Sads."

"What?" Peggy burst out. "Are you crazy?"

"It's just like you said to Gavi. I'll talk to them. If they get to know me and hear me out, maybe I can help them find some hope again."

"But, Molly —"

"I have to," she said insistently. "It's the only way I can

think of to stop this awful crying in my head! Because if I don't do something soon, I'm afraid I'm going to become ... just like them!"

Peggy was devastated. She couldn't imagine having to go on alone. She counted on Molly to have courage enough for both of them. It felt to Peggy as though half of her very self was being ripped away.

But she could see there was no arguing with Molly about this. The doll had seized on this idea to calm her inner turmoil, and her mind was made up.

"Okay, if that's what you have to do," she finally said.

"Will you be all right?" Molly asked.

"Sure." Peggy affected a breezy tone. As horrible as she felt, she was determined not to let on to Molly. "Don't worry about me. Go on. I'll be fine."

Molly threw her arms around Peggy's neck and hugged her tightly, something she hadn't done since Peggy was little. Then she pulled away quickly and disappeared into the darkness on the path.

✧

Peggy found herself singing some of the sea shanties Sir John had taught them back on the *Terror*. It helped take her mind off the biting cold as she made her way down the spiralling path. She told herself it was easier having only herself to worry about. But she kept finding herself turning to make a comment to Molly or Gavi, momentarily forgetting they were gone.

The sense of crushing aloneness grew more intense as

she descended deeper into the cavern. She felt tears burning in her throat as the images of Mi, Gavi, Molly and Jackpine floated through her mind, and then, more dimly, of her mother, her brothers, her room at home — scenes from her other life, which now felt unfathomably distant.

How long had she been walking? How far had she gone? She had no idea. She was only aware that the spiral path seemed to be growing smaller, and that the walls of the great Hole felt closer together. But where did it end? How far was the bottom of the funnel?

She became aware of a feeling of overwhelming dread, which seemed oddly familiar, as though it had been lurking inside her all along, underneath her other emotions.

Then she saw them.

It had been so long since she'd been able to see anything clearly in this godforsaken Hole — other than jagged walls and the narrow path — that she didn't trust what she was seeing. But it certainly did look like a pair of glowing eyes peering at her out of the pitch-blackness.

They were eyes, but they weren't looking at her. They didn't even seem to see her, or anything else. They were blank, hollow-looking.

She called out. "Who's there?"

No response. Not so much as a flicker of awareness of her presence.

She tried calling out again, introducing herself and explaining what she was doing there. Still no sound. She realized to her astonishment that there were many other pairs of eyes scattered all through this zone of the Hole. But all, without exception, exhibited the same blank stare. As she was able to make out more of the faces, she could see that all their mouths were frozen in an open position, but no sound came out.

She tried calling out again, but her voice caught in her throat.

These poor Souls were beyond ranting or crying out in pain. It was as though they were frozen in a state of terror. Now Peggy was gripped by a nameless dread for her own soul. She felt a desperate longing to flee the Hole, to go back to her old life, to wipe Notherland and everything that had happened there from her memory.

It was all over. Their grand effort to save Notherland had come to nothing. Now she, Gavi and Molly were all in the Hole at the Pole. The Nobodaddy had them exactly where he wanted them. They'd walked right into his trap, just like Jackpine before them.

She fell on the path and cried out.

"Let me out of here! I want to go back to my life! I want to go home!"

Exhausted, she collapsed against the walls of the cavern. They felt oddly yielding, as if they were made not of ice but of soft earth. She noticed that the terrain underneath her had the same earthy, yielding quality.

Then something strange happened. Deep in the Hole at the Pole, in the completely soundless zone of the Frozen Souls, she heard a voice, an ordinary-sounding human voice.

Peggy opened her eyes. She wasn't in the Hole anymore. She wasn't even in Notherland. She was sitting on a small grassy hill surrounded by trees. The sun was shining on a nearby pond, and a short distance away from her there were people walking, talking, feeding the ducks ...

She was standing in the middle of Green Echo Park.

CHAPTER 11

Reluctant Hero

AT FIRST SHE THOUGHT she must be hallucinating. She was sure any second now the park, and everything in it, was going to disappear. But the trees stayed firmly rooted to the ground and the gentle breeze made ripples on the surface of the pond.

Is it possible? Have I come back? Just like that?

She was overcome with joy. But that quickly turned to unease. Something was not quite right ...

It's ... warm!

She was in Green Echo Park all right. But there was water on the pond, not ice. The trees were in full leafy bloom. It had been a winter day when she'd left, and now it was summer. What was happening? Could she have been gone that long?

What is going on here?

She tried to calm her growing sense of anxiety. Everything would get back to normal soon, she told herself. She just had to find out what day it was, what time of year, to somehow place herself in reality, this reality.

Don't freak out. Don't attract attention. Just act normal.

She noticed a man standing nearby. She decided to ask him the time, then go and see if she could find a newspaper with the date. She went towards him, trying to act casual.

"Excuse me ..."

He ignored her and threw a stick high in the air. His dog raced to fetch it, barking excitedly.

"Excuse me, I was wondering if you could tell me the time."

The man still took no notice of her.

Weird, she thought. Maybe he was deaf. She tried placing herself right in his line of vision, but he seemed to look right through her, as if she weren't there.

Finally the man turned and whistled to the dog, who bounded over to his side. They both brushed right past Peggy.

"Hello?" she said.

Now she was annoyed. He seemed to be pointedly ignoring her. She called after him even more insistently.

"Mister! Hello?"

She ran over to the dog and bent down, looking right into the animal's eyes.

"Hey there! Hey!"

Nothing. Not a flicker. A shudder went through her. *The dog does not see me.*

Something was horribly wrong. This world in which she found herself now looked like her world, but it wasn't. It couldn't be. Could it?

She thought of her flute. Was it still there on the mound? She felt desperate to find *something* the way she'd left it. If she found the flute still there, maybe things would start making sense again.

She raced towards the ring of trees. But as she approached it she stopped dead in her tracks.

A little girl was sitting on the ground. Peggy didn't want to frighten her, so she held back, straining to see if there was anything that looked like her black flute case on the ground nearby. Then an eerie feeling crept over her again.

There was something familiar about this child.

What is she doing?

The girl was holding what looked like a doll in her lap. She appeared to be fidgeting with something on its head.

Oh my God ...

Now the little girl stood up, clutching the doll. Just as she was stepping out of the ring of trees, something fell to the ground. The girl didn't notice it and ran off.

"Wait!" Peggy couldn't help calling after her. "You dropped something!"

But the little girl didn't seem to hear her. She kept on running, heading out of the park towards the houses on the other side of the street.

Peggy went over to the mound to see what the girl had dropped. Near the trunk of one of the trees was a tiny ball, like a marble. She picked it up and held it to the light.

It was a doll's eye.

She opened her mouth to scream, but no sound came out. It was like in a dream.

I've got to get out of this park. It's making me crazy!

She raced towards the park gate. As she passed under the

stone arch at the gate she thought she heard her name called.

"Peggy!"

She whirled around.

There was no one nearby. The park was nearly empty.

"Peggy!"

"Who said that? Who's calling me?"

"You still don't know?" the voice replied.

Peggy saw no one.

"Where are you?"

"Right in front of you."

Just before her was the statue of the angel. She realized with a start that she recognized the angel's face. Now she recognized the voice as well.

"Lady Jane? Is that you? You've got to help me! All these weird things are happening. What's going on? Why can't people see me?"

"They cannot see you," the voice said quietly, "because you are not here."

"What do you mean?"

"You are nowhere. You are suspended between universes."

"That's crazy!"

"But it is true."

"Why?"

"You are not quite ready to leave Notherland, nor are you ready to return fully to your own world. You are here, but not here."

"But none of that was real! There is no such place as Notherland. It's just some place I made up when I was a kid! This is where I belong."

"Little fool!" the voice now took on the hard-edged quality that Peggy remembered from earlier encounters with Lady Jane. "Have you learned nothing yet? Stop carrying on like a baby! Accept your responsiblity for Notherland. What happens there affects countless other worlds and other lives, not just yours."

"I have no idea what you're talking about."

"When you created Notherland, you tapped into a well much deeper than you could possibly know. Gavi is right — there are many universes. Notherland is only a small part of a vast realm beyond time and space."

"So? What does all that have to do with me?"

"You are the Creator."

"I am so sick of hearing that!"

Now the voice softened a bit. "Yes, I know you are. But you can defeat the Nobodaddy, and you must."

"That's fine for you to say! Who are you, anyway? I can hear that your voice is like Lady Jane's, but you're not really her. You're Sedna, the sea monster, aren't you? You broke up the Everlasting Ice."

"It is true that I assume many guises, but in all of them I am a Resolute Protector of Souls."

Peggy felt her voice grow suddenly small.

"What did you call yourself?"

"I am an Eternal. I have always been and always will be. Did you not know that? Could you not feel my presence?"

Peggy shook her head.

"Well, here I am."

"Fine, if you're a protector, then why don't you protect

me? Why are you trying to make me go back to that place?"

"You still do not see, do you, what I have tried in so many different ways to show you. You have created a great and wonderful story! And the hero of that story is you."

"What if I don't want to be a hero!" Peggy cried.

"But you cannot give up now! You have just found the very thing you need to defeat the Nobodaddy."

"I have?" said Peggy. "Where?"

"There, in your hand."

She was still clutching the doll's eye.

"What, this? It's just an old doll's eye. It was Molly's. She lost it years ago. I just found it ... over there."

"Once a lost thing has been found," the voice said, "it is transformed. It has new properties it did not have before. Molly's eye has become an Aya, an all-seeing eye. Used properly, it can disable the Nobodaddy. Light that is swallowed up in his Hole cannot escape, but an Aya is different. It will retain its illuminating powers even in the darkness of the Hole. And the one thing the Nobodaddy cannot tolerate is being seen as he really is. If you shine the Aya on him, he will be overcome with terror. That should be enough to release the inward pull of the Hole long enough to let the Nordlings and the other Souls escape."

"Oh, great. I go down into his Hole, where he's all-powerful, and this is all I've got to fight him with?"

Peggy's sarcasm was lost on the Eternal, who continued speaking with utter seriousness.

"Yes. If you beam the Aya at him long enough, you might even be able to burn through his heart of ice, the true source of his power."

"Look, you can give me all the good-luck charms you want. It's not going to make any difference. I'll never be able to stand up to him. I don't have it in me."

"No one is truly powerless in the face of evil. Not if we choose to fight it. The important thing is to be ruthless in the service of good."

"Even if I could, what if I don't want to? What if I just want to go back to the way things were before?"

"Then you are free to do so."

"You mean that?"

"If that is your choice, you may return to your life as you knew it."

"I'm sorry to let you down. But yes, I want to go home."

Suddenly Peggy felt a sharp *swish*, like a paper fan whipping through air. Until now the statue had stood utterly immobile, but she watched in amazement as one of its wings, then the other, lifted up in a grand swooping movement. The two huge, magnificent wings slowly came back down and enveloped her within their folds.

For a moment she was too astonished to speak, or even move. Then she realized that the wings felt soft, and she began to lean forward, burrowing into them. The sensation of being cradled in the wings gave her a deep feeling of safety that seemed to reach right to her very core. She wished she could stay there forever, in that place she had so longed to be.

After a few moments, the wings began to move away from her, lifting upward and sweeping down again to the angel's sides. Peggy looked up. The face was impassive again, a statue's. She reached over and touched one of the wings. It was stone hard.

Suddenly she felt a rush of cold air. In front of her face she could see her own breath in swirls. There were shouts, laughter and a familiar swoosh.

She looked out on the pond. It was frozen solid.

Skaters!

Was she back? Was it possible? Was the nightmare really over?

Yes!

Peggy burst out laughing with joy. Some people lacing up their skates by the pond looked over at her.

They can hear me!

Now she laughed even louder. She didn't care if they thought she was crazy. And she remembered something.

My flute!

Was it still there? She ran to the mound. There, lying on the ground at the base of one of the trees, was the black flute case. She picked it up and started waving it jubilantly in the air.

"Woo-hoo!"

She felt as though she'd been snatched from the jaws of hell! Her life had been given back to her. Now she could pick up where she'd left off. And for starters, she was going to head straight back to Around Again with the flute!

She headed out of the park. It was growing dark. Though it had been mild during the day, the temperature was rapidly dropping. Just outside the gate she passed someone huddled in a sleeping bag on top of a sidewalk grate.

"Spare change?"

Peggy looked down. It looked like the Native guy she'd seen earlier, the one the kids had called Scary Gary. In her state of heightened joy and relief, she felt a deep pity for him. She reached into her pocket to fish for some change to throw into the cap he'd set out on the sidewalk in front of him.

She felt something smooth and round among the coins. It was the doll's eye. Strange. How could she still have it, if everything had been put back to the way it was before? Peggy willed herself not to think about it.

Everything's fine now. Everything's back to the way it was.

The young man looked up at her as she dropped a couple of quarters into the cap. His skin had turned an ashen grey in the cold, and his lips were swollen and bluish. He mumbled a faint thank-you. For a moment Peggy met his gaze.

It was the face of Jackpine.

He began to curl back into the sleeping bag. On one of his hands Peggy could see a whitish area, the beginning of frostbite.

He might not make it through the night.

She knelt down next to him. "Do you know me?"

He looked away listlessly, as if he hadn't heard. She reached out and took his face in her hands.

"Do you know me?" she asked again, looking right into his eyes. "Gary? Jackpine?"

For a moment she thought she saw a flicker of recognition cross his face. Then the light seemed to go out of his eyes altogether. Nobody home. Peggy knew instantly where she'd seen eyes with that terrifying emptiness: deep in the Hole, in the zone of the Frozen Souls.

She began to shake him by the shoulders.

"Talk to me! Say something!"

When she let go, his body slumped back into a heap. A cold fury surged through her.

"Don't give up!" she shouted. "Don't you dare give up on me!"

She left him and raced back through the darkened park, to the ring of trees. She stepped onto the mound and began shrieking at the top of her lungs.

"I changed my mind! I'm going back! Do you hear me? I changed my mind! I want to go back!"

Nothing happened. What to do? On impulse, she put the flute case down on the ground, in the same spot she'd found it a few minutes earlier. Maybe if she left things exactly as they were before, she'd be able to go back. The flute had been sitting there waiting for her just now. She'd just have to trust that it would still be waiting when she got back next time.

With a jolt she felt the earth give way beneath her. She closed her eyes.

When she opened them again, she was kneeling on the spiral ledge, in the very spot she had left a short time ago.

The air around her was bitingly cold. She knew she'd have to move fast and keep moving, just to stay alive.

She began to race down the path. After only a few steps it came to an abrupt halt. That was it. No more ledge. Now what was she supposed to do? There was no way to go any farther into the Hole.

No way, except ...

Peggy took a deep breath, stepped off the ledge and plunged into the blackness below.

CHAPTER 12

The Bottom Below

"WHERE IS SHE?"

"Why doesn't she come?"

"What good can she do anyway?"

"Pay-gee is the Creator!" Mi fought to make herself heard over the chorus of grumbles. "She is the one who can defeat the Nobodaddy! And she *will* come! I know she will! But in the meantime we have to keep singing."

"Why?"

"Why bother?"

"What difference does it make whether we sing or not?"

"Because our voices are all we have left!" Mi countered firmly. "Wouldn't you rather fight back than just give up? Sing!" she commanded. "Sing and don't stop!"

Slowly a chorus of notes began to echo through the dark. The Nordlings' voices were weak and dispirited, but at least she'd managed to get them singing again.

Mi was exhausted. She was beginning to wonder how much longer she could keep them going. Even as she put on a brave face for the rest of the Nordlings, inside she felt embattled. She was on the edge of being swamped by dark feelings, the same overwhelming sense of despair that had washed over her as she was wrenched away from the mast of the *Terror*.

But she had to fight those feelings. She couldn't let the others see that she was plagued by the same doubts and questions they were: Where was Pay-gee? Why hadn't she come yet?

Would she ever come?

❖

Peggy felt herself falling, falling. There seemed to be no end to it. She was beginning to wonder if maybe there really was such a thing as a bottomless pit.

As she tumbled downward she began to hear faraway sounds, voices. She wondered if they were the cries of still more Souls trapped deep in the Hole. But as the voices grew louder and louder, she realized that they weren't crying, they were singing.

She landed with a thud on a solid surface. She stood up quickly and was relieved to find she wasn't hurt at all. But the singing had ceased. What happened? Had she just imagined it?

A collective gasp seemed to come right out of the walls of the Hole.

"Light!" She heard voices whispering all around her.

"Light!"

"Light!"

Peggy looked down. The doll's eye, the Aya, was emitting a beam of light in between the fingers of her clutched hand. The Eternal had been right about that much, at least.

Gradually, her eyes adjusted and she began to make out the tiny spirits. They were Nordlings. Some she could see, many more she could only hear, but they were numerous. They had been in complete darkness for so long they could only gaze at Peggy and the light of the Aya in utter amazement.

Excited cries went up.

"Mi was right!"

"The Creator!"

"We are saved!"

"Mi said she'd come!"

"Pay-gee!"

"Pay-gee, the Creator, has brought Light!"

Then they all gathered round her and started speaking at once.

"Hey, hey! One at a time, please!" Peggy asked.

"Let Re9 speak," a voice called out. "He understands more than any of us."

"Yes, Re9!" several others agreed as one of them stepped forward.

"We are overjoyed," Re9 told Peggy. "When Mi came with the news that Pay-gee the Creator was on her way to rescue us, we were afraid to get our hopes up. But she promised us that you would come, and now here you are."

"Mi! Where is she?"

A tiny voice spoke up eagerly. "Here I am."

Mi bounded out of a cluster of Nordlings and rushed over to Peggy, throwing her arms around her.

"We were so worried about you!" cried Peggy, hugging her tightly.

"I'm sorry. I know I shouldn't have gone up in the crow's-nest by myself." Mi pulled away and looked around. "Where are Gavi and Molly?" she asked anxiously. "Aren't they with you?"

Peggy reassured her they were farther up in the Hole, that they were all right and she'd be seeing them soon.

Re9 broke in. "What is that, in your hand? How does it emit light down here?"

"No time to tell you now," Peggy replied briskly. "But if I can just get close enough to shine it on the Nobodaddy, I think it might weaken him long enough to get you all out of here."

"Yes!" said Re9 excitedly. "That would work. Now we just need to figure out a way to get it down into the Bottom Below."

"Isn't *this* the bottom?" Peggy asked.

"Oh, yes," Re9 replied. "This is the bottom, but there is a Bottom Below the bottom."

"Well, that makes about as much sense as anything else in this place," Peggy said. She was starting to feel re-energized. She'd made it this far. She'd found Mi and the rest of the Nordlings. She was ready for anything the Nobodaddy could throw at her.

"How do I get down there?" she asked.

Re9 gasped. "You are not thinking of going down there yourself!"

"Sure. How else am I going to shine this thing on him?"

"But the Bottom Below is the source of the Hole's inner pull, the seat of the Nobodaddy's power. To go down there is to risk total obliteration. No one has ever dared enter the Bottom Below."

"Well, guess it's time somebody did," Peggy replied. "Unless you've got some other bright idea for how I can get close to him."

Re9 shook his head slowly. "I am afraid I do not ..."

Suddenly they heard a kind of swishing noise, accompanied by waves of bitterly cold air.

"Shhh!" Re9 hissed. He lowered his voice to a whisper. "We must be very quiet so he does not suspect anything. There is an opening ..."

"Where?" Peggy whispered back. "How do I find it in the dark?"

"Just follow the trail of the cold."

As he spoke, another blast of cold air began to circulate through the cavern. It seemed to go deep into Peggy's bones.

"There is one thing that worries me ..." Re9 said hesitantly.

"What's that?"

"If you are successful and the pull of the Hole starts to lessen, the Hole itself may start to contract. The opening at the top might begin to seal off."

"How do you know that?"

"I have had a long time to study the physics of the Hole," replied Re9. "According to my theories —"

"That's okay, I'll take your word for it." Peggy smiled to herself. No wonder Gavi called Re9 his star pupil. "I'll just have to work really fast. As soon as you feel the pull start to let up, even a little bit, you've got to go scrambling up the Hole as fast as you can. All of you. And tell the others farther up!"

"We will," he said firmly. "But what about you?"

"Wish me luck," she said as she slipped off into the darkness.

✧

The thrill of finding the Nordlings had encouraged her for a time. But now, as she set off alone, Peggy felt a terror in the pit of her stomach.

She tried to make out where the opening was. She knew she didn't dare use the Aya to find it. As she moved through the cavern it became clear to her what Re9 meant by the "trail of the cold." She crept stealthily in what she hoped was the right direction, while the great swirls of frigid air around her grew more and more biting. Finally she reached down and her nearly numb fingers curled around the edge of some kind of crevice in the cavern floor.

She'd found the opening.

She had to move quickly. The crevice seemed so narrow she wondered how she could get through. She leaned forward a bit more and found herself being pulled downward as she tumbled through the opening head first.

The surface she landed on was oddly soft and yielding, with a rippled texture that seemed to quiver and vibrate, almost like living tissue. It made a strange, unsettling contrast with the stone-cold hardness of the rest of the Hole. The quality of the cold was different here, too — a clammy dampness that threatened to send her into uncontrollable shivers.

So this was the core of the Hole at the Pole, the source of its implacable inner pull. No creature, other than the Nobodaddy himself, had ever come down this far before. She held her breath a moment. Had he sensed her presence yet? she wondered. What would he do? How would he react?

Work fast, she reminded herself. She reached into her pocket and felt around for the Aya. Odd. She'd put it right there. She rummaged around, jamming her fingers into every corner.

Please God, make it be in here somewhere!

All she could find was the little bone flute.

The Aya was gone! It must have fallen out when she tumbled down into the Bottom Below.

What's the matter with you? she berated herself. *How could you be so stupid? Can't you do anything right?*

She began to look for it on the ground. She figured that she ought to be able to make out at least a tiny beam of its light. She prayed the Nobodaddy wouldn't notice it first.

Desperately she scanned the darkness, until finally she thought she could make out a faint pinpoint of light a short distance away. Oddly, it wasn't low down, but more near her own eye-level. Maybe the Aya had fallen onto some kind of ledge that she couldn't make out in the darkness.

She moved towards the source of the light and reached out, and she felt a surge of relief when her hand made contact with something hard. But as she ran a finger along the surface of the object, she realized that it was larger, rougher than the Aya.

Suddenly a harsh, rasping laugh rose up in the cavern and

echoed inside her head.

"*HAHAHAHAHAHA!*"

Peggy quickly pulled back her hand. It wasn't the Aya she had touched, it was ice — the ice of the Nobodaddy's frozen heart.

Now she'd given herself away. The advantage of surprise — the only one she'd had — was gone. The echoing laughter rose up again, accompanied by a cascade of harsh, spiteful words that sounded as though they were right inside her head.

"*Some Creator! You're pathetic! You're nothing! You're worse than nothing!*"

She remembered what Jackpine had said about the Nobodaddy — that being in his presence was like being invaded, that you heard his voice as if it were your own. Was this was what he was talking about? Were those her thoughts or the Nobodaddy's?

"*You're nothing! Nothing! NOTHING!*"

Now the words were all garbled together, a terrifying roar inside her. For a moment the only thing she could think of was getting away, out of range of the horrible voice. She wanted to race back and find the opening, to claw her way out of the Bottom Below. But she couldn't give up. She'd fight the voice by sheer force of will. She had to find the Aya!

Don't listen! she told herself.

She thought she could make out a tiny glint of light, just below where she had reached out. It could be his icy heart catching the reflection of the Aya, she reasoned. Maybe the Aya was hidden somewhere in the soft, rippled ground near where she was standing.

Her eyes scanned the darkness. It had to be just below her somewhere! But she still couldn't see it. She decided she'd have to go down on her hands and knees and grope around until she found it.

She knelt down on the soft, yielding surface of the Bottom Below and stretched out her hands as far as she could reach. A swirl of cold air hovered over her for a moment, then began to envelop her like a cold, clammy mouth. The sensation was repulsive.

She forced herself to keep looking for the Aya. But she began to feel a profound exhaustion wash over her. She tried to shrug it off but it grew stronger. It felt as though her spirit, the very thing that gave her the will to keep going, was slipping away.

The Nobodaddy was sucking the life right out of her.

She felt herself growing weak and listless as her hands scrambled frantically. She was desperate to find the Aya before all energy was drained out of her.

Then the harsh laugh began again, along with the volley of words, now so loud they felt like a continual pounding inside her head.

"YOU ARE NOTHING NOTHING NOTHING ..."

It was too much. Why had she come here? Why had she been foolish enough to believe that she could stand up to something so powerful?

"Give up. It's useless to keep fighting. Just give up."

Maybe this is what dying is like, she thought. *Or something even worse than dying. Death-in-life.* She collapsed to the ground.

Something momentarily jolted her — a sensation of something small and hard, right under her left hip. Was it the Aya? A pebble? A chunk of ice? She had no idea. By an enormous effort of will she shoved her hand underneath her hip and grasped the object. Then, using all the strength she had left, she flipped onto her back and held it out above her.

The Nobodaddy screeched in agony as a blast of light hit him full in the face.

"AAHHHHHHHH!"

He sprang backwards, out of the range of the Aya's beam, shrieking with rage.

She sought out his position in the darkness, shining the Aya in the direction of the roaring voice. But every time the light caught him, he managed to jump out of its range.

He began to recover his forces and laughed his cruel, taunting laugh again.

Peggy realized with a growing sense of panic that there was no way she could hold the light on him long enough to get a clear picture of what he looked like. All she could make out were snatches — an arm, a tuft of hair, a flash of eye. And if she couldn't keep him in the Aya's beam long enough, what good was it? Without a steady, strong source of light, how was she supposed to weaken him?

The laughter roared around her, ricocheting off the walls of the cavern. Then a terrible thought occurred to her.

How long would the light of the Aya last?

What was she supposed to do now? Things were at a standoff. The Eternal had promised her the Aya would do the job. Why hadn't she warned Peggy about this?

She decided she had to do something else to try and keep him off balance. But what? The only other thing she had with her was the bone flute.

She remembered what Gavi had said when they had first set out on their journey: *"He does not hear it as music at all, the way we do, but as a horrible, grating noise."*

She'd dismissed it as more of his empty theorizing. But what if he was right? Could this primitive little flute be a weapon she could use against the Nobodaddy?

At this point, anything was worth a try. She reached into her pocket and pulled it out. She lifted it to her mouth with one hand, still aiming the Aya with the other. She covered the holes with her fingers and blew, holding the note long and steady.

Do ...

She uncovered one of the holes and blew again.

Re ...

Then she lifted her finger from the other hole and blew.

Mi ...

As the notes resounded through the Bottom Below, a terrible screeching rose up. At first Peggy had no idea what it was. She kept on playing, worried that the flute's notes might not cut through the volley of sounds.

Do ... Re ... Mi ...

The more she blew, the more intense the screeching became. Finally, she realized it was the Nobodaddy himself making the sound. He was wailing and groaning, like someone crying out in intolerable pain.

It was so terrible listening to his agonizing moans that for a moment she was tempted to stop playing. But she recalled

Jackpine's words: *"You can't hesitate ... You have to go after him ... Maybe hatred is something you could use a bit more of ..."*

She blew into the bone flute with renewed intensity. The screeching turned almost plaintive, like a child's piercing wail. Was it working? Was the Nobodaddy growing weaker the longer she played? She didn't dare stop, even for a second. How long could she keep it up? Would the Aya hold out? If only she had more light!

She thought she could hear another faint, faraway sound — not the bone flute, not the Nobodaddy's screeching, but something else. Whatever it was, it was growing louder, and now she could tell it was coming from above her.

A sudden blast of light hit her in the face. She looked up to see the Nordlings flooding into the Bottom Below, one after another. Peggy shone the Aya on each one as it entered the cavern, which seemed to have the effect of intensifying their light, making each one even brighter.

Soon the Bottom Below was flooded with light. Peggy could scarcely believe what she was seeing. Then more words of Gavi's popped into her head: *"Light increases light. That is one of the basic laws of Notherland."*

She swore she'd never doubt him again!

Still singing, the Nordlings boldly formed a circle around the Nobodaddy. As Peggy flashed the Aya around the cavern, it began to produce an almost kaleidoscopic effect. As each one of the Nordlings grew brighter, it was as if the RoryBory itself had been brought right into the bowels of the Hole at the Pole.

For the first time, Peggy managed to get a glimpse of the

Nobodaddy's face: it bore an expression of pure terror. The Nobodaddy was paralyzed, overwhelmed by the light.

She aimed the Aya right into the centre of his heart of ice, and the intense beam began to burn a hole right through it. He let out a piercing howl, and for a moment she turned the beam away. Her momentary hesitation allowed him to snap him out of his paralysis. He began taunting her again.

"*HAHAHAHAHAHAHAHA!*"

Now she recalled the Eternal's words: "*The important thing is to be ruthless in the service of good.*"

She lunged forward and stabbed the Nobodaddy in the heart with the jagged end of the bone flute. And the heart began to shatter, tossing shards of ice everywhere as a hissing sound rose up from it. She lunged at him again and again with a seething fury that grew more frenzied with each thrust of the jagged bone. So this was what hatred felt like — a coldness, a hardness gripping her own heart, almost as though it were turning to ice, like the Nobodaddy's.

Finally she felt a hand on her arm. It was Mi.

"Peggy, stop."

"Look!" some of the other Nordlings shouted.

They all stood and watched in amazement. The Nobodaddy was finally fully visible. It was a strange sight, and Peggy finally understood why she hadn't been able to make out any of his features with the Aya. For he seemed to have no single form. His shape was constantly changing. Sometimes he had an ugly, even monstrous, aspect; then he would take on the appearance of an ordinary human — sometimes male, sometimes female. Peggy realized that as they looked on, the Nobodaddy was taking on the form of every loved one he had assumed in his lifetime as a soul-stealer.

It was then that Peggy realized that the hissing sounds were no longer coming just from the the disintegration of his icy heart. Before their eyes, the Nobodaddy was shrinking, losing form, collapsing into himself. The hissing was the release of all the energy that had been trapped inside him. Peggy and the Nordlings watched, aghast, as the once-powerful entity grew smaller and smaller, compressing into a ball, until it was no more than a tiny, nearly invisible, speck of matter.

The Nobodaddy was returning to his original essential form: Nobody.

Just at the point where his features began to dissipate into utter formlessness, the Nobodaddy released one final, horrifying, vengeful roar that shot up from the Bottom Below and echoed through the great cavern of the Hole at the Pole.

❖

Gavi had managed to get the Mads to stop yelling at one another long enough to hear the great roar.

"What was that?" they asked each other. They all turned to Gavi.

"I am not sure ..." he said slowly. "If it is what I hope it is ..."

Lower down in the Hole, the Sads, at Molly's insistence, were all huddled together, both for warmth and to help bolster their spirits. Some were whimpering softly. A few had stopped crying altogether when the great roar resounded.

They were frightened but curious, and they showered Molly with questions.

"What was that noise?"

"Why did it stop?"

"Is it a bad sign?"

Molly's voice came back firm and confident in the darkness.

"Of course not, it's a good sign! It means we'll be getting out of here any minute now!"

Even farther down, none of the Frozen Souls reacted to the great roar, except for one, a young man. At first, as the fierce noise resounded through the Hole, his eyes, like the others, registered nothing. But something, perhaps snippets of images that felt like memories — a tree, a young woman, a bird, a ship — stirred his consciousness. As he began to blink his eyes, the sound finally registered in his brain.

His tears began to flow, and for the first time ever, a cry rose up in that part of the Hole, so searing and heartfelt that it even managed to rouse the other Frozen Souls out of their barely alive state.

❖

The reverberations of the great roar finally died away. For a moment there was an eerie stillness in the Bottom Below. Then, like an elastic band pulled taut until it finally snaps, the walls of the Hole began to vibrate and shoot inward.

The Nordlings screamed, terrified that they would all be crushed to death. But just before the walls around them collapsed, Peggy and the sprites, suddenly released from the Hole's downward pull, felt as though they were being propelled upwards. They were pulled through the opening of the Bottom Below and up into the main part of the Hole. As they careened through each zone, they were joined by the other prisoners — the Frozen Souls, the Sads and the Mads — till they were all shooting upwards in a great mass. Behind them, the walls of the Hole continued to collapse and snap together, pulling the Hole into itself, making it narrower, shallower.

Peggy kept looking up anxiously. Could the opening of the Hole have already sealed shut? If so, they would all be crushed when they reached the top. She thought she could make out the opening above her, with a spot of blue sky showing through. But she could see that, as the crowd of Souls drew nearer the top, the opening was growing smaller and smaller.

The top of the Hole was closing, just as Re9 had speculated it would. She could only pray they would all get out in time.

First out of the opening were the Nordlings, the lightest and fastest, even though they'd had the farthest to go. They shot through the rim in a cluster, and as they landed on the perimeter of the Hole, they began to dance and shout with wild abandon. The rest of the Souls came spilling out in a great mass, whooping Mads mixed in with laughing Sads, trailed by the still-stunned but awake and aware Frozen Souls.

The last out were Molly, Gavi and, finally, Peggy. The three of them fell upon one another, laughing and hugging. Molly and Gavi started to ask Peggy how she'd managed to overpower the Nobodaddy, but she pulled away, her eyes frantically scanning the crowd.

"Where's Jackpine? Do you see him anywhere?"

Molly looked. "He must be around here somewhere."

"Then why can't I see him? Where is he? Maybe I was too late!"

"Too late for what?"

Peggy didn't answer but called out into the crowd.

"Jackpine? Anyone know him or where he is? Jackpine!"

Most of the Frozen Souls had been huddling off to one side. After being trapped so long in the Hole, they were frightened by the expanse of open space around them, and their eyes weren't used to the brightness of the sun. Out of their midst a young man emerged. He looked weak and walked slowly, but he had a mischievous grin on his face.

"Who's looking for him?"

Peggy let out a gasp. "There you are!"

They ran towards one another, and Peggy impulsively threw her arms around him.

"I'm so glad you're okay!"

"Me too!"

He lifted her up and swung her around joyfully for a moment. Their faces touched and their lips nearly brushed against each other's. As he put her back on her feet they both looked down, slightly embarrassed, and out of breath.

"We did it," Peggy said.

"You did it," he corrected her. "I gave him a pretty hard time, but you're the one who got us all out of there."

She looked into his grinning eyes, relieved to see that the light had come back into them. A shudder ran through her as she thought back to the sight of Gary — his stricken expression, his ashen-grey face, his frostbitten fingers. Jackpine had no idea just how close to death he'd come in the world on the other side of Painted Rock.

He looked at her and seemed to be on the verge of saying something more. But they were distracted by a loud rumbling behind them. Everyone turned and watched as the upper-most walls of the Hole at the Pole finally collapsed in on one another. It vanished, leaving no trace except a kind of circular scar on the hard black ice where the rim had been.

There was an eerie silence as the Souls took in the enormity of what had just taken place. Then a huge, pro-longed cheer rose up.

The nightmare was over. The Hole was gone.

CHAPTER 13

The Shining World

AS SIR JOHN HAD PROMISED, the ship was "at the ready." Now the old captain watched with growing excitement as the great mass of Souls, led by Peggy, made their way across the ice shelf to the *Terror*.

"Well done!" Sir John effused, as they streamed onto the ship. As Peggy, Jackpine, Molly and Gavi boarded, he beamed and saluted each of them in turn.

"This was among the most dangerous missions I have ever commanded. If we were heading back to England — which we are not, a fact with which I am now fully at peace — I have no doubt that Her Majesty would be decorating you all with medals of the highest order! Very well done!"

When the last of the Souls had finally boarded, Sir John gave Molly the order to pull up anchor. The *Terror* began to inch forward out into the open water, its sails billowing in the wind.

"Excellent," he said to his newly augmented crew. "The winds are favourable. Let us be on our way."

But the Souls just stood in clusters, staring back at him.

"Well? What is it?"

"Where are we going, sir?" ventured one.

"We want to go back to the lives we had before," said another. "Will this ship take us there?"

Sir John was flustered.

"I ... I'm not entirely sure ..."

Peggy bounded up onto the foredeck.

"We're heading south to a spot called Painted Rock. There's a very thin border there between Notherland and the other world. That's how you're all going to get home."

"Are you sure?" someone called out. "Has anyone ever crossed that barrier?"

"I have!" she replied with conviction. But she could see some of them were sceptical. Before they could ask any more questions, she heard Molly's voice.

"Look!"

Huge, jagged columns and boulders of ice were slowly moving through the Great Polar Sea, right in their direction.

The icebergs. Of course. They should have been ready for them!

"Molly! Take the helm!" Sir John called out, gearing up for another round of frantic manoeuvring. But when Peggy looked out over the *Terror*'s bow, she was astonished to see that none of the huge ice-forms was in the ship's path. They had completely moved out of the way, forming a long line on either side of the ship.

The icebergs, it appeared, were letting the *Terror* sail through unharmed, as if offering a kind of silent homage.

The ship continued on, flanked by the icebergs, until it was evening. Awaiting them at the end of the formation was an even more wonderful sight — the Great Skyway.

All the Nordlings burst into joyous song at the sight, which none of them, save Mi, had laid eyes on for a long time. One by one they eagerly bounded up the slide and sought out their familiar places on the RoryBory. When they were all in place, the RoryBory became a spectacle of light, the intensity of which had rarely been seen before.

"It looks like a stairway to a shining world," said one of the awestruck Souls watching from the deck of the *Terror*.

✦

All through the next day, the *Terror* made its way through the Great Polar Sea, labouring mightily under the weight of its human cargo. Gavi, Peggy and Molly were concerned about Sir John's reaction to this unaccustomed activity, but he patrolled the ship beaming with pleasure.

"It does my heart enormous good," he told them, "to see the *Terror* once again put to good service."

As they sailed, Gavi eagerly delivered explanations for the events they'd witnessed and expounded on other matters of philosophy. Most of the Souls didn't have a clue what he was talking about, but they listened with rapt attention. How brilliant he was! Molly and Peggy smiled at each other; Gavi had found a fresh audience for his theories.

There was a great deal of merrymaking above and below deck — singing and dancing to tunes played on homemade instruments, which seemed to appear out of nowhere. At times things got a bit rowdy, especially among the Mads. Some of them fell back into their old combative ways, and it took stern words from Gavi and the captain to bring them into line. Even worse were a few of the Sads, who began to wonder out loud if they would ever get back home.

"Have we been freed only to wander aimlessly on this enormous sea?" they asked.

Molly gave them a stirring pep talk.

"Listen to yourselves! You sound as if you were still down in the Hole!"

Secretly, Peggy worried — what if the Sads were right? Could she get them all back to the other world? She'd failed once before. What would be different now?

And there were other, more immediate problems to deal with — namely, what to do about the Frozen Souls? Most of them were very young children, and their adjustment to life outside the Hole was proving more difficult than anyone had anticipated. They tended to huddle in small groups in the darkest areas of the ship's hold, afraid to believe their ordeal was really over. Molly and the others tried to coax them to come up on deck, to dance and sing, or just listen and be part of things. But they held back.

"What are we going to do?" Peggy asked the others. "It's like they won't let anyone get near them."

"They've got their reasons," Jackpine volunteered. "Leave them alone. They'll come out when they're ready."

Later that evening, the Nordlings were playing and scurrying around the deck, trying to avoid their bedtime ride into the night sky. The Great Skyway hung suspended, reaching right down to the deck of the *Terror*. Some of the bigger Nordlings would pretend to start up the Skyway, only to slide back down again, giggling. Because of all they'd been through, Gavi and Molly just smiled at their hijinks. Soon all the Nordlings had joined in the silliness, starting up the Skyway and sliding down again, most of them laughing uproariously.

Finally, Molly put her foot down.

"That's it. Playtime's over."

"Awwwww," they chorused, but they were soon distracted by Mi, pointing in the direction of the stairway to the hold. A few of the rescued Frozen Souls had poked their heads through the opening, and were watching the goings-on intently.

"Would you like to play with us?" Mi asked.

Molly began to object, but Peggy stepped forward and gestured to Molly to leave them be.

The little Souls looked at one another silently for what seemed like a long few moments, until at last one of them nodded.

"Come on," said Mi, holding out her hand.

They crept out from the stairway and walked over to the Great Skyway, eyeing it warily. Then they clambered on and started upward, imitating the Nordlings. One of them, a tiny, wide-eyed boy, finally stopped, turned around and slid down the Skyway, laughing all the way. The others followed his lead, and giggled softly as they tumbled downward.

Drawn by the sound of their laughter, the other Frozen Souls began to stream up from below deck. They, too, began to scamper up the great slide and tumble down, whooping and laughing. The Nordlings, perched at various points on the Skyway, watched the whole drama with keen interest. Then they all joined the throng of little Souls sliding down the Skyway.

Molly groaned. "How are we ever going to get them to go back up?"

✧

The next morning they reached the Everlasting Ice. Sir John and Molly steered up and down along the edge of the ice shelf several times, hoping to find some pathway through it. But there was no trace left of the Warm Line, nor any other broken-up patches. As far as they could see, there was nothing but a vast expanse of solid, unbroken ice.

"I believe it will be necessary to moor the *Terror* here and continue on foot," observed Sir John briskly. But Peggy could see they'd come to a point in the journey that Sir John had privately been dreading. The prospect of leaving behind his ship — his long-time home, his last link with his beloved Jane — filled the old seaman with an overwhelming sadness.

Peggy watched Sir John with unease. Even if they did manage to get back to the other world, what would become of him once they were gone? Gavi, Molly and the Nordlings would all stay behind, too, of course. But Sir John needed a focus, a sense of purpose. Where would it come from now that their mission was complete?

"Look!" one of the Nordlings suddenly called out, pointing out on the ice. "What's that out there?"

Everyone on deck turned to see an astonishing sight.

Out on the Everlasting Ice sat Lady Jane Franklin. She

was seated on a chair, beside which was a small table and another chair. The table was set with a full tea service, and Lady Jane was serenely pouring tea from a fine china pot.

No one uttered a word as Sir John walked slowly over to the edge of the deck and looked out over the ice. After a moment, Peggy and Jackpine went over and gently helped the old man climb down. They watched as Sir John walked slowly and gingerly, so as not to trip on the slippery surface.

When he reached the table, Lady Jane looked up at him and smiled warmly. She nodded to her husband to sit down, and leaned across the table to pour tea into his waiting cup. For a long time, the two of them sat drinking tea and conversing, their voices carrying in a low murmur across the expanse of ice to the ship.

Night began to fall. When the Great Skyway made its appearance and touched down to the edge of the deck, the Franklins stood up. Sir John leaned over to pick up a small object from the table, then took his wife's hand as they slowly walked back to the *Terror*.

The Nordlings were uncharacteristically quiet and solemn as they gathered at the base of the Skyway, readying themselves at last for the trip upward. As the old couple approached the ship, Lady Jane raised her hand, gesturing to them to hold off their departure. The two of them stood near the Skyway, and Sir John turned to Lady Jane with a look of rapturous happiness. Then, unexpectedly, he broke the silence, calling out Molly's name.

The doll bounded quickly over the side of the ship and went hurriedly to the old man. He smiled and saluted her.

"Ensign Molly," said Sir John, "in the name of Her Royal Majesty, I hereby promote you to the rank of captain. You shall now take command of this vessel."

Speechless, Molly could only salute back. The old captain leaned forward and gave her a great bear-hug. Then he held out the object he had picked up off the table and handed it to her.

"So that you will remember me. So that the world will remember Franklin."

He turned to Peggy, Jackpine, Gavi and the great gathered mass of Souls on the ship and raised his arm in a long, heartfelt salute.

Lady Franklin gestured graciously to the Nordlings to start up the Great Skyway. She took Sir John's hand, and the two of them also began to ascend, surrounded by the shining beams of the Nordlings' light. Even before they had assumed their places in the RoryBory, a great chorus swelled to fill the night sky.

Peggy watched the old couple grow smaller and smaller as they made their way upward. She knew that in the morning the Nordlings would, as usual, make their way back down to earth, but that this was the last they would see of Lord and Lady Franklin.

They had gone up to the Shining World.

"Look." Molly was holding out the object Sir John had given her.

Peggy stared at it, amazed. It was a silver teaspoon — the same one she'd found in the park, the one from the picture in *Our Wondrous North*.

"I found that spoon in the park!" she told Molly. "But that was before I came here. So how come you ...?" But her voice trailed off as the memory of the Eternal's words came back to her: *You tapped into a well much deeper than you could possibly know. There are many universes.*

✧

What to do about the *Terror*?

Peggy slept fitfully during that night, wrestling with the question. In the morning she felt no closer to a solution. But it soon became clear that Molly had been doing some thinking of her own.

"The *Terror* is my responsibility now," she informed Peggy. "What kind of captain would I be if I abandoned her?"

Peggy looked at her quizzically.

"What are you saying? That you're not going on with us? That you're staying behind?"

"No," Molly was quick to reply. She wanted to finish the journey with the others. But once they arrived at Painted Rock and passed through into the other world, she would return to the *Terror* with her crew and take up her new mission — to patrol the Great Polar Sea and safeguard Notherland from evil entities.

"Wait a minute." Peggy stopped her. "Crew? What crew?"

Molly, it turned out, had spent much of the night seeking out recruits from the ranks of the Souls. There were quite a few who, on reflection, decided they didn't want to even attempt to return to the other world, who felt their lives and futures were here in Notherland. Captain Molly had given them a sense of purpose, a reason to remain, and so they'd readily agreed to serve under her on the crew of the *Terror*.

"I'll whip them all into shape in no time," she said firmly. "There won't be any lollygagging on *my* ship!"

Once she'd had a chance to get used to the idea, Peggy had to admit that it made some sense. But she had one big concern.

"What about Gavi? What does he say about all this?"

"I haven't told him yet," Molly admitted.

"It's a little hard to picture Gavi living out his days on a ship," Peggy said. She could see that the same thing weighed on Molly's mind, too. "Let's not say anything to him just yet."

"Okay," Molly agreed. "But won't he figure something's up when ...?"

"When what?"

Molly swallowed hard.

"When we ... rename the ship."

Now Peggy was really taken aback.

"Rename the ship? Why would you want to do that?"

"I know you don't just go changing a name for no good reason," Molly replied hastily. "And I wouldn't dream of insulting Sir John's memory. But he made it clear that I was to take command. It's my ship now. And I think ... the name *Terror* is too much of a reminder of what this ship has been through, what we have all been through. I want to start fresh."

Peggy listened to Molly's passionate argument. Clearly the doll was abrim with energy and fresh resolve. And it was true that the name *Terror* didn't seem terribly appropriate anymore. Now that Sir John had himself passed on into Eternity, maybe it was time to let go of the past. Maybe it would help them all step back into life.

"Okay. But what will you call it?" Peggy asked.

"Naming things is your job," Molly replied. "You're the Creator, remember?"

As they prepared to leave the ship, Molly called everyone together. One of the Souls retrieved an old bottle made of thick, heavy glass from the galley below. Peggy filled it with water from the Great Polar Sea and held it out to Molly. But the doll shook her head.

"Have you chosen a name?"

Peggy nodded.

"Then you do the honours," said Molly.

They all stood facing the great ship.

"I hereby rechristen this vessel Her Majesty's ship ... *Resolute*."

She smashed the bottle against the side, and it shattered into tiny glistening shards, which showered onto the ice below.

❖

Now they had to make their way across the Everlasting Ice on foot. But as soon as they began to work up a brisk pace, they found themselves slip-sliding on the slippery surface. Molly called to Peggy and Jackpine.

"Come on. Let's show them how to do it!"

She grabbed each of them by the hand, and the three of them broke into a sprint, which sent them into a long skid across the ice. Others followed suit, and soon the air was filled with laughter as more and more Souls began racing across the ice in long, sliding strides.

"Yipppppeeee!"

Soon Molly broke away to join some of them in a game of crack-the-whip. Peggy extended her arm and felt ripples of excitement when Jackpine took her hand in his. They moved side by side in silence.

Some Souls picked up the gliding movement easily, but Peggy looked back and noticed that a few were having difficulty. She reluctantly dropped Jackpine's hand to see if they needed help. They were grumbling that it was too hard to cross the ice, that Peggy was making them do it. Peggy was taken aback. It drove home to her the uncomfortable fact that, though she was surrounded by all these Souls, she was really alone. The Eternal had told her that being the hero would be hard; what she hadn't told Peggy was that it would, at times, be crushingly lonely as well.

She was seized with an intense longing to just be herself again. She was weary of all this responsibility, of carrying all the weight on her shoulders. She didn't care about being the Creator. She was tired of being a hero. She wanted her life back — she wanted to see her mom, her friends at school, even her annoying brothers. She ached to go home.

She remembered how she'd felt that night before her journey into the Hole, and how she'd cried out her sadness on the bone flute. She felt for it in her pocket; it was still there. And for the first time since that strange, brief trip back to Green Echo Park, she thought of her other flute, the one she'd been so eager to get rid of. Was it still where she'd left it, waiting for her?

✧

When Molly spied the shimmering waters of Lake Notherland in the distance, she let out a whoop of joy and dashed ahead. Gavi, however, was distant, subdued. He lumbered to the shore, slid his black-and-white body onto the surface of the water and swam out into the middle of the lake, seemingly lost in thought.

For Peggy, the sight of Painted Rock as they rounded the shore of the lake stirred up a mixture of anticipation and anxiety. This was the moment of truth. She'd saved them all. Now, would she be able to get them all back home?

As they approached the rock, Peggy looked back at the Souls following behind her. They were all waiting for her to say or do something. She hoisted herself up onto a nearby rock and began, awkwardly, to speak, gazing at her friends.

"I guess this is goodbye. I wasn't crazy about the idea of coming to Notherland in the beginning. But now I'm glad. Because I might not have gotten to know any of you." She was afraid to look in Jackpine's direction as she said this. "We're about to go our separate ways now. But I hope none of you forget who you are and what we've been through together. You've been down to the bottom of the Hole at the Pole and come back out again. I hope that, if any of us manage to meet up in the other world, we'll somehow just know one another. Now — let's all go home."

She jumped down, stood squarely in front of Painted Rock and concentrated. In her mind's eye she tried to picture the surface of the rock growing transparent, so that she could make out the landscape of the park on the other side. But when she opened her eyes nothing had happened. She closed her eyes and tried again.

Panic rose as she opened her eyes and realized there had still been no change. After all she'd done, all they'd been through, was this how it was going to end?

Make it work this time, please!

She tried again.

Nothing.

Peggy turned to them all, defeated.

"I'm sorry. It's not working. I don't know what else to do."

There were angry shouts from some of the Mads.

"I knew it! I knew we'd never get out of here!"

"We should never have trusted her!"

Then another voice pierced through the angry shouting.

"Quiet!"

Peggy turned. It was Jackpine.

"Good thing she didn't rely on the likes of you, or you'd all still be down in the Hole!" he chided them. "Now shut up and give it a chance."

Jackpine walked over and stood up close to Painted Rock.

"What are these?" he asked, pointing to the red markings on the rock.

"I don't know," Peggy replied. "They've always been there."

He stood pensively, running his fingers over the markings.

"What is it, Jackpine?" Peggy asked.

"I can't explain it, but these markings look familiar somehow. Like I've seen them before."

He traced one dark red line with his index finger.

"Right, of course. See? This is a drawing of a tree. And over here. That looks like a canoe with two people in it. This one is strange. It looks almost like an eye."

"An eye?" Peggy said.

Jackpine was right. Though some of the outline of the drawing had faded with time, it clearly depicted a single disembodied eye. The dark-red markings on Painted Rock had always looked to Peggy like smudges, discolorations in the rock. But as Jackpine carefully traced their outlines, she saw for the first time that they were patterns, pictures ...

Now Mi piped up.

"That one looks just like Gavi," she said in her tiny voice.

"This one?" said Jackpine. "You're right. It looks just like a loon."

Peggy was struck by a thought.

"Wait a minute! One of them looks like a loon and one looks like an eye? Maybe ..."

Jackpine seemed to know immediately what she was thinking. "Maybe they all mean something? Like the tree! Don't you see? That's me!"

"And the loon is Gavi," cried Peggy, "and look! These two people — one is taller than the other. That could be me and Molly. And the two people in the canoe? That's Sir John and Lady Jane! Yes! See? It's all of us! I can't believe I didn't see it before!"

"But that was not possible!" Gavi broke in excitedly. "Do you not see? Our whole adventure was foretold right here on Painted Rock, before it ever began! But you could not understand the story until you had lived it!"

"These here look like tiny birds," Jackpine pointed out. "They could be the Nordlings. And this looks like a snake. That's got to be the Nobodaddy!"

"Or it could be the sea monster that attacked the ship!" Molly added.

It could even be the Resolute Protector of Notherland, Peggy thought to herself.

They were all startled by the sound of a great crack! They watched in amazement as a deep fissure appeared in Painted Rock. It widened until it had almost the appearance of a pathway, beckoning to them.

Peggy turned to Gavi.

"What's going on?"

"My best guess," he replied, "is that this is no longer just a pathway into your park. There are so many Souls preparing to cross over, heading for so many far-flung places throughout your world, that something more is needed."

"Do you think it's safe for them to start passing through?"

"We have come this far, I cannot believe we will be thwarted in our mission now."

Peggy sighed with relief. In letting the drawings speak to him, Jackpine had found the way to their freedom. The responsibility for Notherland was no longer solely hers; it wasn't all up to her anymore.

She signalled to the Souls nearest the rock to begin their journey. A small group started through the huge fissure until, at what seemed like a point deep inside the rock, they simply vanished. The rest followed in twos and threes.

Peggy turned to Molly, but the doll was talking to Gavi. She was telling him breathlessly of her plans for the *Resolute* and her fears about his reaction.

Gavi stopped her. He seemed not in the least perturbed, or even surprised.

"Of course you will want to stay with your ship. I would not have expected anything else. But I have something to tell you, too."

"You do?"

The loon looked intently at her, then at Peggy.

"Well? What is it?"

"I am not going to stay on the *Resolute* with you."

"Oh? Where will you go?"

"That is … I am not going to stay in Notherland."

"What are you talking about?" Molly demanded.

"I am going to try and pass through into the other world."

"Gavi, no!" Peggy said. "You've never tried to cross over. You have no idea what will happen to you!"

"But now that so many appear to be crossing over without difficulty, there is no reason why I should not attempt it, too," Gavi replied calmly.

"But …!" Molly sputtered. "You're not from that world! You belong in Notherland!"

"I know, I know. Everything you are saying I have told myself. I have thought it all through. The truth is, I am tired of thinking. I am tired of having to figure everything out. I want to experience life as a flesh-and-blood loon does! I want to bond with a mate. I want to father a loon chick. I want to fly north in the summer and south in the winter. I don't want to just think about life. I want to *live* it."

"But Gavi!" Molly cried. "What about the Nordlings? We've always looked after them together."

"With you and the new crew of the *Resolute* to look after them, I know they will be in good hands, as will Notherland itself. But I cannot live on a ship. There will be nothing for me to do."

Peggy gave him a penetrating look.

"Gavi, it'll be very different for you in my world. Things are in constant change there. Everyone grows older. Here in Notherland, you're protected from all that. You're immortal. If you cross over with us ..."

The loon nodded.

"I will die one day, like any ordinary loon. Yes, I have considered that, too. But if death is the price of fully experiencing life, it is a price I am prepared to pay. After seeing Sir John and Lady Jane pass over into Eternity, I have no fear. I am ready to dive headlong into the great pool of existence."

Molly tried to stifle a sob.

"But ... you might never be able to come back," she finally said. "We might never see one another again."

Peggy's eyes, too, were starting to burn with tears. With all that had been on her mind the past few days, she'd managed to block out all thought of saying goodbye to these two, but now the reality of it was finally coming home to her.

"I do not wish to leave you, anymore than you wish to leave me," Gavi said gently, tears filling his eyes. "We are being called to different paths, in different worlds. But we will always carry one another in our hearts."

At that moment, Peggy looked out over Lake Notherland and saw a column of silvery-blue light. It grew brighter and brighter as it settled right over the Nordlings, bathing them in its glow. Then it spiralled out and formed an enormous ring encircling them.

"I have always been and always will be. Could you not feel my presence?"

Peggy remembered the Eternal's words, and now knew for certain that Notherland still had its Resolute Protector.

Molly's voice broke in on her thoughts. "It's time!"

Peggy turned back towards Painted Rock. Jackpine was standing alone at the entry to the passageway; all the other Souls had passed through.

Gavi reached the opening first. As he started to move his cumbersome body into the passageway, he looked back at them.

"Do not be surprised to find a loon swimming on your pond when you arrive on the other side," he said to Peggy.

Swimming? Peggy abruptly stopped him. "Gavi, wait! It's winter back in my world. There'll be ice on the pond."

"Then you must help me take off, so I can migrate south."

"But you've never migrated anywhere! How will you find your way?"

"I will follow my .... my instinct!" the loon said with pride.

Then he turned to Molly.

"Take good care of our beloved Nordlings, Molly. Goodbye."

Biting her lip, the doll walked hesitantly forward and held out one stiff arm. Her hand grasped one of Gavi's wings and squeezed it hard. She was determined not to let herself start crying again.

Silently, she mouthed one word to Gavi: *Goodbye*.

Then he disappeared into the passageway, releasing one last tremolo as he went.

"Till we meet *agaaaaiiiiinnn* ..."

Once he was gone, they heard a low rumbling in the earth around them.

"What's that?" asked Jackpine.

"My best guess, as Gavi would say," said Peggy, "is that the opening between the worlds is starting to become unstable."

"We better get going before it gets any worse!"

As they turned to say goodbye to Molly, Peggy suddenly thought of something. She reached into her pocket. Nestled in a corner next to the bone flute was the Aya. She took it out and quickly pressed it into Molly's hand. The doll looked at it in amazement.

"What ... But this is ... How did you find it?"

Peggy grinned at Molly.

"It's a long story," she replied.

Peggy wanted to say more, but the rumbling was growing louder. There was barely time for Peggy to give the doll one last hug as Molly pushed them both towards the opening.

"You two get out of here!" yelled Molly. "Now!"

Jackpine grasped Peggy's hand. In the narrow passageway their bodies were pressed close together, their faces so close they could feel the warmth of one another's breath. What would happen when they crossed over? Would he even remember her? Would she remember him?

This might be my last chance! she thought.

She leaned over and pressed her lips to his for one long moment.

As they both went tumbling through the passageway, she could swear she heard Jackpine's voice, saying her name.

"Peggy, I ..."

Then everything went dark.

Epilogue

ALL THROUGH THE DAY Souls had passed through the portal. The fissure in Painted Rock had narrowed but not yet closed up completely. Now, with night falling, Mi discovered that, from her spot on the RoryBory, she could watch everything that was happening on the other side. She suddenly thought again of Sir John talking about the parting of the Red Sea. She realized, with regret, that she'd never gotten around to asking him how a sea could be red.

She had to fight to stay awake. But seeing into another universe was so exciting!

There was a crowd of people gathered in what Pay-gee had called a "park." They were talking animatedly and pointing towards a body of water much smaller than Lake Notherland, but with a smooth surface of ice.

"Can you beat that?" Mi heard one of them say.

"Yeah, it's something, isn't it?" said another. "A loon, here, in December."

A bird was slapping its wings on the surface of the ice with a restless, fevered motion.

"Maybe it was too stupid to fly south for the winter," said another, and laughter rippled through the crowd.

"Now what's that girl up to, do you suppose?"

A young woman was striding purposefully out onto the ice. She looked a lot like Pay-gee herself, but with a difference that Mi couldn't quite put her finger on. She walked right over to the bird, put one arm around it and started to gently pull it along the ice. The bird made no effort to resist or escape her; it seemed to grow oddly calm at her touch.

"Is she crazy?" someone in the crowd exclaimed. "She's liable to scare that bird half to death."

"Maybe not," said another. "Looks like she's trying to pull it to the far end of the pond, so it can have more room to take off. That's why the poor thing's flailing around like that. It can't take off. Loons are like big planes — they need a long runway to get up enough speed."

There was a minor commotion in the crowd as the girl was joined by someone else, a young man who reminded Mi of Jackpine. But she thought she might be mistaken when one of the people on shore pointed at him.

"Hey, there's Gary, that Native kid who hangs around here."

"Now y'know they're *both* crazy," chuckled someone else.

It wasn't clear to Mi whether the girl who looked like Pay-gee and the boy who looked like Jackpine knew one another or not. But together they tried pulling the bird backwards, then vigorously pushing it forwards, away from them. The loon's wings began to flap furiously. The bird managed to propel itself partway across the pond, then its momentum slowed. The two young people ran over to the bird and repeated the same action, pulling it backwards with a running motion, then thrusting it forwards even more vigorously.

This time the loon skittered across the entire length of the pond, picking up more and more speed as it went along. Just as it approached the opposite bank, its black-and-white body finally began to lift off the surface of the ice.

The crowd watched the loon pass over the edge of the pond and begin to gain altitude, until it was soaring in the sky over their heads with long, steady wing strokes. Spectators broke into spontaneous applause as the loon soared higher and higher, until it was little more than a tiny black speck on the horizon.

Mi watched the boy and girl walk off the ice together. At the edge of the ice, the girl picked up an oblong black box. She opened it, took out a long silvery object and began blowing into it. The crowd stood listening, enraptured by the sound, as Mi was, too. She had never heard anything quite like it: music, but not like that which Mi and her companions sang in the RoryBory. Beautiful music, full of energy and delight. The music of another universe.

Finally the fissure in Painted Rock closed up completely and Mi couldn't see anymore. But she could still hear the music from the strange silvery instrument as it trailed off into a faraway echo.

From her place in the blazing RoryBory, Mi looked down from the sky over the vast sweep of Notherland. In the distance, off to the north, she thought she could make out the *Resolute* moored at the edge of the Everlasting Ice.

Maybe tonight, she thought as she drifted off to sleep, *I will dream a new universe into existence.*